Brutal Ter

Brutal Terminations

Cherith Baldry

Matador
9 Priory Business Park,
Wistow Road, Kibworth Beauchamp,
Leicestershire. LE8 0RX
Tel: 0116 279 2299
Email: books@troubador.co.uk
Web: www.troubador.co.uk/matador
Twitter: @matadorbooks

ISBN 978 1788038 089

British Library Cataloguing in Publication Data.
A catalogue record for this book is available from the British Library.

Typeset in 11pt Minion Pro by Troubador Publishing Ltd, Leicester, UK
Printed and bound by CPI Group (UK) Ltd, Croydon, CR0 4YY

Matador is an imprint of Troubador Publishing Ltd

In Memory of Group 13
Oxford 1969-71

'...civil rites that take off brutal terminations.'
Sir Thomas Browne, Urne-Buriall, Ch 4

All the quotations at the chapter headings are taken from the works of Sir Thomas Browne.

Chapter One

'Than the time of these urns deposited, or precise antiquity of these relics, nothing of more uncertainty.'

Urne-Buriall, Ch 2

A peremptory knock came at the study door of the Dean of St Clement's. Dr Stephen Verner, the Dean, growled, "What now?" *sotto voce*, and aloud, "Come."

The door opened and Edwin Galbraith, the Master of the College, strode into the room. "These bones," he said without preamble.

Verner, who was trying to write a paper on the financial difficulties of the Third Crusade, clicked the 'save' icon on his laptop and pushed himself back from his desk with a disapproving glare at the Master's pin-striped neatness. His nose twitched at a whiff of expensive aftershave.

That morning the workmen who were digging the foundations for the new extension to the college library had unearthed a skeleton, driving the whole College into a flurry of academic dismay.

Once the police had been called, Verner would have preferred not to give his mind to the macabre discovery, but knowing the Master's well-known propensity to meddle, he recognised that he did not have that option. "Well?" he growled.

"The police are out there."

"I know."

"They've put a kind of canvas screen thing round the… the hole." The Master's plump, well-kept hands sketched a vaguely rectangular shape. "They're all in there, but I don't know what they're doing, and they won't tell me."

Considering resignation to be the better part of valour, Verner reached for his pipe and began stuffing it with evil black tobacco. He wished, silently, that the Master would take himself off and concern himself with his own research – whatever that might be.

"I can tell you what they're doing," he commented.

"Did they tell you – " the Master began, ready to take offence.

"Of course not, Master. Use your common sense. They'll be taking photographs. Then they'll have to get it – him – out, and I expect they'll sift through the soil and take samples to make sure nothing else is there."

"But – "

The Master paced agitatedly towards the window and peered out, quite uselessly, since the site in question was on the other side of the college. "But surely, Dean, these are old bones?"

"Old?"

"Antique." Blinking, as if he realised that he had perhaps not chosen the best word, he amplified. "Historical. Relics."

Verner shrugged. "Why ask me?"

"You're a historian, for goodness' sake!"

There was a brief silence as Verner lit the pipe, and his reply was punctuated by vigorous puffing that sent clouds of smoke billowing into the room. "Certainly, Master, if you…want information on…the finance of the early Middle Ages. Bones not my field. You want Templeman… archaeologist."

"I can't find Templeman, dammit!"

"Try Bodley," Verner suggested hopefully.

The Master failed to take the hint. Instead he started skittering about between window, desk and door. Even the pipe smoke did not seem to discourage him, much to Verner's disappointment, but at least it disposed of the appalling reek of aftershave.

"The police could be doing untold damage," the Master said peevishly, obviously reminding Verner that it was he, when the site foreman had first reported his workman's discovery, who had insisted on calling them. "That might be a valuable site. A burial or something. Templeman will never forgive us."

Verner, hunched over his pipe, scratched a reflective ear. "It is undoubtedly a burial," he stated. "But of what antiquity… You realise, Master, that these might be quite recent bones?"

Although the Master halted, pivoted, and stared at him with every appearance of horrified surprise, Verner was fairly certain that he had been entertaining this idea all along. Never a man to confront unpleasantness, the Master clearly preferred someone else to shoulder the burden of putting it into words.

"You mean – a body?"

When, Verner wondered, did a body stop being a body and become a historical relic? When were the police content to hand over to the archaeologist?

"No, no, Verner, absolutely impossible." The Master

was babbling. "Think of the College! Think of the scandal!"

Verner thought. It was, of course, highly undesirable that a body of recent vintage should have been deposited in the St Clement's College gardens. It would be almost certain that a member of the College should have been responsible for so depositing it, and maybe – even worse – responsible for its being a body (dead variety) in the first place. A scholarly, therefore inquiring, mind could hardly refrain from asking, "Who?" Verner did not want to have to answer. He had been a member of College himself for almost forty years.

He had the sense not to pass any of these thoughts on to the Master, merely saying peaceably, "We must wait for the police report."

"But they won't report! That's what I'm trying to tell you. And meanwhile – " The Master started pacing again as he unloaded another grievance. "The builders can't get on with the job, and who's going to pay for the delay, that's what I'd like to know!"

Verner brightened. "You'll have to take that up with the Bursar."

"He isn't here either," the Master complained. "His wife rang in. Stomach upset."

"Sorry to hear that."

"It would have to be today of all days. When we need men of authority..." The Master's voice and expression both contrived to suggest that for some reason Nemesis was lying in wait for him and that at any moment the College might crumble into its constituent elements. It was a mood Verner was familiar with; at such times the Master was apt to consider anyone's defection as a personal affront.

"I don't suppose he had much choice in the matter," Verner said, feeling vaguely sympathetic towards the absent Bursar.

There were members of College for whom 'stomach upset' might be simply a euphemism for 'hangover' but in the case of the energetic and efficient Colonel Morrison, it probably was a stomach upset. Verner hoped he could have it quietly and quickly somewhere else and that he himself could avoid having to discuss it.

To his relief, the Master seemed prepared to drop the matter, absolving the Bursar from the evil intent of deliberately being ill on the day the College discovered these questionable bones, and took his leave, though he paused at the door to deliver himself of a parting, or Parthian, shot. "This would have to happen just before the College Gaudy!"

"Cancel it," Verner said; there was no sign, as the door closed, that his advice had been heard.

He turned back to the financial problems of Richard I, who had said, engagingly, that he would sell London if only he could find a buyer. But the Dean's concentration had been broken. Although he essentially despised the Master, as a businessman but no scholar, Verner could not help feeling that he had a point. If the newly discovered bones were indeed not merely bones but remains to which a personality might be attached, then the College was up to its collective neck in trouble, and might be regarded, not only by the police, but by the Press and by the various funding bodies on which the College depended, much as the people of Rome had been regarded by Caligula. Nasty, however you looked at it. Unfortunately, the problem would not go away just because the Master declared it impossible.

Verner smoked silently for a few minutes longer, and then reached out for the telephone.

The receiver at the other end was lifted almost immediately. A light voice, recognisable, though less familiar than it had once been, said, "Gawaine St Clair speaking."

"Verner here, Stephen Verner." A well-bred question mark seemed to hover in the air. "Dean of St Clement's."

A second's silence. Then: "Of course. Do forgive me. What can I do for you, Dr Verner?"

Verner launched into the story of his – or the College's – bones. Gawaine listened without interrupting, and when Verner had finished there was silence again.

"Are you there?" Verner barked.

"Of course. I was just wondering, Dr Verner, what possible reason you could have for ringing up to tell me all this."

Verner bristled at the languid voice coiling its way down the line. As if he didn't know!

"What worries me," he explained, "is what happens if we have a dead body in our garden. What if the police start probing?"

"What have you to hide?" Gawaine inquired.

"Damn it, you know that everyone has something to hide. This College no more nor less than most. Look, St Clair, we're scholars – most of us – we don't know how to handle the police. I'd be very grateful if you would come down and hold a watching brief on behalf of the College."

The silence this time was even longer. As it continued,

Verner was able to examine exactly what it was he was asking. He could picture Gawaine, or at least picture the undergraduate he had been not all that long ago, the negligent charm masking an alert intelligence and an unexpected bedrock of integrity. Except that now the mask was carefully cultivated, and if there was any way of reaching what lay beneath it, Verner had not discovered it. He could only think of Gawaine as someone who had been involved, however coincidentally, in other affairs quite as messy as this. He had read about them in the kind of newspapers the younger dons left lying around the Senior Common Room. It was perfectly clear to Verner that no sane man – and Gawaine, although undoubtedly eccentric, could not be called certifiable – would wish to be so involved again. That was what he was asking, and he could think of no earthly reason why Gawaine should agree. Except, perhaps, out of loyalty to the College. And what, Verner asked himself silently, did we ever do for him?

"And when would you like me to come?"

Verner started visibly. It had been a long shot; utterly impossible that it might actually have hit the target.

"Soon as you can."

There was another hesitation, but a short one. "This evening, then. Always supposing that the traffic doesn't do something perfectly frightful. Once can never entirely trust the M25, don't you agree?"

And after the exchange of a few more civil amenities, he rang off. Verner sat staring at the telephone for so long that he allowed his pipe to go out. Grunting, but more in surprise than irritation, he tried to give his mind once again to the problems of Richard Coeur de Lion.

*

When he had put the receiver down, Gawaine St Clair sat motionless at the Sheraton desk in his study. The torn-up card inviting him to the College Gaudy was still in the bin beside him. His adroit avoiding of St Clement's hook had been quite futile; all it had required was different bait. Briefly he closed his eyes and murmured, "No." Then in his turn he reached out for the telephone.

Chapter Two

'But who were the proprietaries of these bones, or what bodies these ashes made up, were a question above Antiquarism.'

Urne-Buriall, Ch 5

David Powers steered his sports car down the slip road and onto the M25, neatly overtaking an airport bus on its way to Heathrow. A swift glance at his passenger showed him that Gawaine had closed his eyes, presumably to contemplate the eternity he feared he might be facing.

"Don't worry," David said cheerfully. "I've never totalled a car yet."

"There's always a first time," Gawaine murmured.

"So tell me about this body," David went on as he settled into cruising speed. "Why are your dons freaking out like this?"

And they're not the only ones to be freaking out, he added silently to himself. He knew how much Gawaine hated the times when he became involved with murder, but his phone call that morning – the attempt at insouciance behind which David could discern blind panic – was something entirely new.

"Bones, rather than an actual corpse," Gawaine replied pedantically. "For all we know, they may be archaeological relics."

"Then isn't it a bit soon for everybody to start panicking?"

"I suppose so." Gawaine let out a long sigh. "But if the bones are recent, then the College can expect some very nasty publicity."

"My heart bleeds." As the satisfied graduate of a red-brick university, David had little interest in dreaming spires. Especially now, when the thought of returning to Oxford had obviously thrown Gawaine badly off balance. His usual airy affectations were subdued, and his expression, in spite of his valiant attempts to hide his feelings, betrayed deep apprehension.

"Are you sure you want to do this?" David asked him. "I can turn off at the next junction. Just say the word."

"I'm not sure, but..." Gawaine shook his head and added with an attempt at a light-hearted tone, "I must not leave undone those things which I ought to have done."

An exemplary upbringing had made David familiar with the words of the Book of Common Prayer, though it was years since he had heard them. But all that meant something to Gawaine, he knew, and was maybe at the root of his refusal to back away from affairs like this, however unpleasant they promised to be.

"But are you sure?" Gawaine continued after a moment. "I know it's a fearful imposition – "

"We went through all that on the phone," David interrupted. "It's fine."

"But you should be at work..."

"That's all sorted," David told him. "I'm working from home."

"But you aren't at home," Gawaine pointed out plaintively.

David rolled his eyes. "I have my laptop, and that's all I need," he said. "I assume your College has wifi, or do they still communicate with a bit of parchment wrapped around an arrow?"

He was gratified to hear a murmur of amusement from Gawaine. "Home is where the laptop is... Yes, of course there's wifi. No expense spared."

"Then there's no problem. At least until the end of the week – though let's hope these bones are relics and we can wrap the whole thing up right away."

"*Occidit, occidit spes*," Gawaine commented.

Latin was all Greek to David, but Gawaine's sombre tone told him all that he needed to know.

For all Gawaine's misgivings, David avoided all erratic pantechnicons, inconveniently sited trees and speed cameras, and the bright scarlet car slid across Magdalen Bridge in the heavy sunlight of late afternoon, to make a left turn into the lane that ran alongside St Clement's.

David parked and followed Gawaine along a high wall of grey stone and through a wide arched entrance into the porter's lodge, a medieval gatehouse of the same grey stone. There was a rack of pigeonholes at one side, a couple of abandoned bikes leaning against the wall and a later addition of panelled wood and glass where the porter had his lair.

When David entered Gawaine was already in conversation with the porter: a small man, wizened though not old, with a bright eye and an ingratiating smile.

"...exactly like old times," Gawaine was saying.

"You haven't changed a bit, sir."

Gawaine flicked a rather desperate glance towards David, and replied with what he was obviously meant to say. "Neither have you, Heatherington. How are the children?"

"Well, sir, my son, he's married now. He's working with these computers, doing very well. And my daughter, she's up at the House, reading Physics."

"Excellent news," Gawaine responded. He was preparing to go on, with a nod and a faint smile, when Heatherington asked, "Was you wanting the Dean, sir?"

"Yes."

"You'll find him in his study, sir, same as always. I'll ring through and tell him you're on your way."

Energetically he began to crank a handle attached to a switchboard of unimaginably antique design, and Gawaine was able to escape.

"I suppose that means," he murmured, "that the whole of College knows I'm here, and why. Or if not, they soon will. Heatherington always was a frightful old gossip."

He led David across a stretch of garden and into the college buildings through an iron-studded oak door that might have guarded the entrance to Castle Dracula. Gawaine threaded his way confidently through a maze of dark-panelled corridors, and finally stopped and tapped at a door. A voice from inside growled, "Come." Gawaine opened the door and ushered David into the presence of the Dean of St Clement's.

Even David, fresh from life in the fast lane, felt that it was a presence. Stephen Verner was an elderly scholar, with shaggy white hair and eyebrows tangled over eyes that looked at you rather as he might have surveyed a pile of floor sweepings in which he had possibly, but not probably, lost a coin. He was also the scruffiest man David could remember seeing in a long time, though it was an aristocratic scruffiness. The ancient tweed jacket with leather patches on the elbows had been good once, long ago…

David came to himself as he realised he was being introduced.

"I hope you don't mind that I brought David," Gawaine said. His voice was light, affected, his barriers up; there was no sign of the disquiet he had betrayed on the way. "Absolutely indispensable, I promise you."

Verner swivelled and glared at David. "Not a member of this College?" he barked.

"No," Gawaine replied. "Nor of this University. Actually…" He spoke with delicacy, as a cautious chess player might advance a pawn. "…he's in advertising."

The glare intensified. "Advertising?"

The Dean might have used the same tone if David had confessed to selling children for the white slave trade. David wondered how many graduates of the College had gone into advertising, or if those with such ambitions were simply dropped into some convenient oubliette.

Meanwhile Verner brushed the whole matter aside, on the principle, perhaps, that if you ignore something unpleasant it will sooner or later go away. "Sherry?"

He reached for a decanter and poured. David took his drink into the window seat, where he could observe without risking too close a scrutiny. The study, he thought, could almost have been a stage set for an Oxford don's hide-out. Books lined the walls and lurked on the floor in piles. Crossed sculls adorned the space above the fireplace and on the mantelshelf was a photograph of a rowing team among whom David recognised a much younger Verner. The large desk was almost invisible under a drift of documents, except from where an up to date laptop rose like an island from the surrounding flood.

Gawaine wilted gracefully into a leather armchair near Verner's desk, losing not a scrap of his customary elegance as he did so. Watching him, David had the uncomfortable feeling that they should never have come within a hundred miles of Oxford – but then, he had known that ever since Gawaine's phone call of that morning. What it was about Gawaine that attracted these affairs was and always would be a mystery to David. Now he was all negligent fragility, turning some nicely conceived epigram on the College wine. The ruffled golden hair and innocent expression combined to give him an air of absolute incompetence.

"Have there been any developments since you rang?" he asked the Dean.

Verner cleared his throat and hunched into his jacket until he had the air of an evil old gnome. "Have there not!" he said. Just before you arrived, I had the police in here, with the preliminary results of the post mortem. It's bad. No, I take that back. It's bloody awful."

Gawaine raised his brows infinitesimally, but otherwise made no response. It was, of course, scarcely gentlemanly to begin wailing and gnashing of teeth, though David had the impression that the Dean might have appreciated a more positive reaction.

Verner cleared his throat again and reached out,

almost as a reflex action, for pipe and tobacco pouch. "The body – " he began.

"Body?" Gawaine interrupted swiftly.

David did not see the reason for the interruption, but Verner obviously understood perfectly. "Yes, body. Not a nice set of archaeologists' relics after all. Mind you, I could see it coming. Why I sent for you."

Gawaine inclined his head, a graceful acknowledgement of the implied compliment. "And the body..?"

"Has been there about thirty years. Not long. Been here longer myself." Verner was tamping down tobacco in his pipe, but had forgotten to light it. "And that's not all. There are some definite facts emerging now, and I don't like them. For one thing, the body was female."

Gawaine gave a slight jerk, and then relaxed deliberately, as if he had been betrayed into an unseemly display of feeling.

"And pregnant."

This time Gawaine's start of surprise was more pronounced, and quite unselfconscious. After a moment's pause, he murmured, "Oh dear."

"Is that all you've got to say?"

"It seems to sum up the situation admirably."

Verner snorted. "Could be right. Just ask yourself how many pregnant females should have been swanning around College thirty years ago – five years before we were dragged kicking and screaming into going co-ed." Before Gawaine could reply, he answered his own question. "I'll tell you. None. Bar the odd married scout. And I'll tell you something else. This one wasn't married."

By now Gawaine had himself in hand again, and there was no reaction but a faintly inquiring look. "Not?"

"No wedding ring."

Silence fell as Gawaine frowned and sipped his sherry, a silence broken by a muttered curse as Verner realised what he had been doing to his pipe. He groped among the litter on his desk until he found a little metal widget and started to scrape it out again, scattering tobacco crumbs all over his shirt front.

Gawaine went on communing with whatever truth he could discern at the bottom of his glass, and David wondered how long it would take him to realise that the situation was quite impossible, so that they could go home.

"No evidence of who she was?" Gawaine asked eventually.

"No," the Dean replied. "Not yet, anyway."

"And no one reported missing at that time?"

Verner shook his head. "No. I was here then, and I don't remember anyone wondering about the whereabouts of their sisters or their daughters. Of course, I wasn't Dean in those days, but I think I'd have heard."

Listening to the conversation, David could not help remarking that Gawaine's air of incompetence somehow seemed to have evaporated, and most of his affectations along with it. He supposed he had no right to be surprised any longer at the change in Gawaine when he was giving his mind to a problem; he had seen it often enough.

"I don't think, Dr Verner," Gawaine said, "that she was anyone's sister or daughter. Not, if you follow me, significantly."

"I follow you." Verner was having another go at the

pipe. "She was somebody's woman, he got her pregnant, she came looking for her rights, so he murdered her and buried her in our garden. And he got away with it."

Gawaine blinked a little at this somewhat crude summary. "Succinct," he admitted. "Is there any evidence as to cause of death?"

"No, not officially. But if she died naturally, what on earth is she doing in our garden?"

That was one question that did not require an answer. Gawaine considered briefly and then shook his head. "I'm sorry, Dr Verner, I don't think I can help you."

"What do you mean, you don't think you can help me? I'm relying on you to tell me who put her there."

Gawaine's frown returned. "Do you really want to know?"

"Of course I want to know! For goodness' sake, this College is heading for a really juicy scandal. All we can do to avert at least some of it is to find out where the blame really lies."

"But Dr Verner, look at the facts. This happened thirty years ago. I don't know how likely it is that the police will be able to identify this woman, but even if they do, how easy will it be to find her murderer? Someone who was here thirty years ago – but he doesn't have to be still here, does he? He could even be dead. And where on earth do you expect me to start? No, Dr Verner, I'm frightfully sorry, but I really don't feel I can be much help."

"Are you running out on me?"

Gawaine stiffened slightly. David felt that this might be the time for him to make a helpful comment – such as the ultimate common sense of returning home without loss of time – but before he could speak, Gawaine replied, "Of course not. I'll stay as long as you think I can be useful."

Verner grunted, a satisfied sound. David reflected that he had been stupidly optimistic to expect Gawaine to refuse anyone, however impossible the request.

"Then I'll take you to meet the Master," Verner said. "You're dining on High Table, by the way."

Gawaine was unimpressed. "The Master?" he queried.

"New since your day. Galbraith. Edwin Galbraith."

"Oh, yes, I seem to remember reading something," Gawaine said silkily. "He came from one of the newer universities…Cambridge, was it?"

For the first time Verner's features shifted into something like a grin. "You've not changed."

The comment drew a rather alarmed look from Gawaine, but no reply.

"The Master, then," Verner continued. "He'll be expecting us." His head turned and he directed an evil look towards David. "You'll probably get on with him like a house on fire."

Chapter Three

'If they dyed by violent hands, and were thrust into their urns, these bones become considerable.'

Urne Buriall, Ch 5

In the bedroom allotted to him by Verner, Gawaine was trying to tie a dress tie, using a mirror that had evidently been put in place by a much taller undergraduate. He was still at it when he heard someone entering the sitting room, and David's voice speaking his name.

David appeared at the bedroom door a moment later. He was already dressed for dinner, having been forewarned by Gawaine before they left. Gawaine suspected that he used a made up dress tie held in place by a piece of elastic, but he naturally had too much delicacy to make the accusation without solid evidence to back it up.

"What did you make of the Master?" he inquired.

David shrugged. "Not a lot. I don't make much of any of them, to tell you the truth. It's not my scene."

Gawaine smiled faintly. "It's very good of you to come, my dear David. I'm very grateful – how could I possibly function without Watson?"

A necessary part of these affairs was his guilt at involving David. If one chose to spend part of one's superfluous time poking around old corpses, that was one thing, but to expect anyone else to tolerate it was quite another.

I hope it's not gratitude. Unwelcome memories pushed their way into Gawaine's mind, of the time when David had been mixed up in an affair quite as messy as this, if not worse. It was the first time Gawaine had discovered his talent – if it was indeed a talent and not a curse – of unravelling the impenetrable tangle of murder. David would have been arrested without Gawaine's intervention, and ever since Gawaine had wished heartily that both of them could forget it.

Thinking back, Gawaine was never quite certain when the balance had swung over from helping David to needing him. All he knew was that without David events would be totally out of control; that was what had sent him panicking to the telephone earlier in the day. He was never quite sure whether his relationship with David justified him in doing that. Flippantly to address him as Watson was no solution.

Somewhere in these meditations the perfect butterfly had formed beneath his fingers, and he reached for his dinner jacket. "What do you feel about Verner's bones?" he asked.

David remained noncommittal. "I don't see what he expects you to do."

"No. It's a comforting thought. I've no idea if she can be identified after thirty years, or if it would be possible to find her murderer – always assuming she was murdered. But if it is possible, it's a job for the police. Tracing missing persons, looking for connections with all the people who were up here at the right time… They have the organisation for it."

"Then why are we here?"

Gawaine raised his brows. "For the good of our souls?" Immaculate now, he led the way to the outer door. "No – so that Verner can feel he's doing something."

"And so that the Master has something positive he can tell the Press?" David suggested.

Gawaine shuddered. "You're probably right." Giving himself a mental shake, he continued, "Tomorrow I'll try to see the police officer in charge of the case, and after that…well, I'm as eager to get out of here as you are, believe me." He paused on the stairs and looked up at David, who was following him down. "Thirty year old bodies are not *my* scene."

David faced the prospect of dinner on High Table with certain misgivings. He had expected, and could cope with, the ambiance – the ancient dining hall, the linenfold panelling, the portraits which were presumably past Masters as opposed to Old Masters. He had expected a certain quality of food and wine, and even to feel, in the case of the wine, that he was not really qualified to judge. He had also expected the conversation of dons, and that was where his misgivings lay. He doubted his ability to keep up with the level of erudite chit-chat that these occasions presumably demanded.

He found himself with Gawaine on one side of him and two empty spaces on the other. Opposite were Verner and a Classics don named Porteus. The Master was a place or two further down. The only other person at all within David's reach was the College chaplain, Father Gerard. David concentrated on effacing himself and listening.

As he tuned in to the conversation, David found that Verner was holding forth on the subject of the empty spaces.

"Morrison's wife rang in," he was explaining, apparently in reply to a question asked by the chaplain. "Stomach upset, so she said. Shouldn't wonder if it was that mutton stew last night."

Father Gerard smiled gently. "That would be the *ragout d'agneau avec –* "

"Stew," Verner snorted. "It would upset anyone. Makes you feel like asking if anyone's seen the College cat lately."

David, finding the topic of conversation rather less elevated than he had been led to expect, surreptitiously prodded the contents of his plate, which he had so far accepted quite happily as chicken, and heard Gawaine murmur, "Courage!" into his ear.

"Can't think what's happened to Templeman," the Dean continued, now addressing the question of the other absentee. "Haven't seen him all day. Come to think of it, the Master was looking for him this morning."

The chaplain – a very old man, round and pink-faced with a shock of wispy white hair that stuck out like a dandelion clock – made a remark about pressure of work.

"Doubt it," Verner returned. "Not out of term. And Templeman likes his glass of wine as well as anyone."

David was conscious that Gawaine had flicked him a glance – meaningful, and at the same time troubled. For the first time he began to realise that the vanished Templeman might well be relevant to their problem. A body is discovered. A don vanishes. Could there possibly be any connection between the two?

David considered the idea and dismissed it. If an old crime was coming home to roost, the best policy of an intelligent man – and dons were presumably intelligent – would be to lie low and say nothing. Only a fool would decamp at this stage of the game.

"Who's Templeman?" he murmured to Gawaine.

"Archaeologist. And rather a nice fellow, actually."

"Was he here when it happened? You know, when she was put there?"

Gawaine frowned, thinking. "Do you know, David, I'm not sure. He's not all that old. Maybe as an undergraduate – "

He broke off, interrupted by Porteus, the Classics don. "St Clair. I've just been trying to place you. You were up – what – eight, nine years ago?" It was a high-pitched voice with a trace of a Northern accent, and it did not sound friendly.

"Something like that," Gawaine replied.

A certain quality in his tone alerted David; for some reason, Gawaine did not want to talk to Porteus. It made David look at the don more closely. He was somewhere in his fifties, tall and sinewy, with dark, receding hair and thin features that seemed contracted into a perpetual sneer. David decided that his acquaintance was something he personally could do very well without. Unfortunately he was, for the present moment, stuck with him.

"Verner says you've come to look at these bones?" Porteus asked.

"If I can help..." Gawaine began.

"Absolute nonsense," the don interrupted. "The police are bound to find a perfectly simple explanation. As I recall, St Clair, you had enough trouble with your own field, without trying to interfere in someone else's."

The attack was so unexpected, so vicious, that David was momentarily taken aback, and before he could say anything – which under the circumstances would have been remarkably stupid – Gawaine was responding in the light, affected tones which told anyone who knew him that he had withdrawn entirely from the situation, leaving a pleasant but mindless persona to carry on in his absence.

"I'm frightfully sorry, Dr Porteus. Of course I shouldn't dream of interfering with the police – too perfectly competent, don't you find them? – or with the College. But the Dean, do you see, seems to think that I – "

"Absolute nonsense," Porteus interrupted again.

He had a pinched, malevolent look about him. David began to think more seriously of intervening, but he was forestalled by Father Gerard.

"My dear Miles..." He patted Porteus's arm, peering benignly at him over half-moon spectacles. "Do stop fussing, there's a good fellow. Or we might think you protest too much. Don't you want the truth about this unfortunate girl to come to light?

Porteus subsided, though still looking displeased. "All I want is to be left alone," he muttered, "and to get on with my work."

The chaplain, to whom David began to think there might be more than met the eye, smiled innocently at Gawaine. "Very nice to see you again, my dear fellow. For whatever reason. Do you get the chance of doing any reading these days? Have you seen the thing Henderson has just published on Pelagius? Complete and utter rubbish, of course. Now in my view..."

David was mildly impressed that Gawaine was capable

of following, and even contributing to, a discussion of the iniquities of whoever-it-was on Pelagius – whoever he was. Giving up entirely, David let the conversation drift around him until it was time to adjourn for coffee. No one disturbed him to ask him for his views on anything whatsoever.

Coffee was served in the Senior Common Room. As they withdrew, Gawaine murmured encouragingly, "Well done, my dear David. Not long now. Come and console yourself with the College brandy."

In the Common Room, another panelled room dotted with armchairs and with a well-stocked bar at one end, David managed to annexe a seat next to Gawaine, and inquired in an undertone, "What was all that about?"

"Pelagius?"

"No. Him –whatshisname – Porteus. Who rattled his cage?"

Gawaine turned on him an innocent, blank expression. "He used to be my tutor. I suppose he found me a frightful nuisance, even then."

That told David nothing, which was clearly what it was designed to tell him, but before he could say any more he was interrupted by Verner, who came by and leant on the back of Gawaine's chair.

"Thought you ought to know," he announced abruptly. "Couldn't tell you in there, not in front of everybody, though God knows, it'll get around soon enough."

"What will?" David asked, irritated.

He received one of Verner's looks, the one reserved for undergraduates patently guilty of indescribable evil. "Just before dinner I had the police on the phone," the

Dean went on. "They've established the cause of death." He paused.

"Yes?" Gawaine said.

Verner protracted the pause a little longer. Then: "She died of a broken neck."

Chapter Four

'Teeth, bones and hair, give the most lasting defiance to corruption.'

Urne-Buriall, Ch 3

The next morning, Gawaine went alone to see the police, leaving David to his own devices, with an appointment to meet for lunch at the Mitre. He was not looking forward to the interview, but he felt that perhaps it was something useful he could do, and afterwards he might make a reasonable excuse to go home. If nothing else, that would please David.

He turned into the police station and identified himself to the sergeant on the desk. Verner had telephoned, so that he was expected. Not long afterwards, he found himself shown into the office of Inspector Carter, the man in charge of the case.

Carter was not there, and Gawaine had time to take stock of his surroundings. The room was bright and functional, with an air of being stripped for action that scared Gawaine stiff. The furnishings were modern steel and glass; the only concession to humanity was a bushy little plant on the desk. This plant Gawaine identified as a specimen of mind-your-own-business – an extremely inappropriate choice to decorate a police station.

Gawaine was meditating on this, and wondering if the plant might possibly be over-watered, when Carter at last arrived. He was tall, thin, fortyish, with greying hair and an ascetic face. In another context, he could himself have been mistaken for a university don.

His reaction when Gawaine introduced himself was slightly surprised, slightly wary. Gawaine had met reactions like that before. He had no illusions about himself, or the impression he conveyed. He was not, he knew perfectly well, the sort of person one could imagine the College choosing to represent their interests. But, he had to remind himself, if any of that bothered Inspector Carter, it was his problem.

"If we're to believe the likes of Agatha Christie," the Inspector began, "England used to be crawling with amateur sleuths. But I have to admit you're the first one that I've met."

"Amateur, certainly," Gawaine responded, deeply embarrassed. "But I'd hardly describe myself as a sleuth. I'm simply holding a watching brief on behalf of the College."

"And pigs fly," Carter retorted. "I've heard about your previous..."

Convictions? Gawaine wondered, as the Inspector searched for a word.

"...exploits," Carter finished. "But this isn't the nineteen-thirties," he went on with a frosty look. "These days the police have access to highly specialised technology and forensics. Why do you think that you can do better without that?"

Gawaine forbore to point out that on several previous

occasions he had done better. "Maybe I can't," he replied. "Nothing would please me more than to leave everything to the police. But...I know the College. And I know some of the people involved. Besides," he went on after a brief hesitation, "it's a whole different world, in there. I might notice something odd – out of place – that you or your staff might miss. And people tend to talk to me. I'm not sure why, but they do."

Carter gave a doubtful grunt. He had, Gawaine noticed, a penetrating look from deep dark eyes, as if something was going on inside his head that wasn't allowed to appear on the surface. The thought wasn't reassuring.

"So you're offering an exchange of information?" Carter asked.

"Exactly."

The Inspector stared at him for a few more seconds, then relaxed. "Whether all that is true or not, remains to be seen," he said. "However, your Dean is very keen for me to work with you, so for the time being, we'll see how it goes. But I'm warning you, step on any toes, and you're out."

"I understand."

That said, Inspector Carter became, to Gawaine's relief, if not friendly, at least co-operative. He sent for the file on the case, and someone produced a fluid roughly approximating to coffee.

"So exactly what do you want from me?" Carter asked.

"If you could just bring me up to date..." Gawaine murmured vaguely. He would infinitely have preferred to discuss the care and maintenance of house-plants, but he could scarcely say so.

Carter flipped open the file. "Right. Deceased was a woman, Caucasian, aged between twenty and twenty-five, blonde – "

"You could tell that?" Gawaine interrupted.

"Oh, yes."

"A bracelet of bright hair about the bone…" Gawaine whispered, shivering.

Inspector Carter looked at him a little harder. "Donne," he said, then added, "And she died of a broken neck," so quickly that Gawaine had no time to react.

"Murdered?" he asked.

Carter shifted in his chair and drank some coffee. Tasting his own, Gawaine wondered if the plant was over-watered because visitors surreptitiously tipped their drinks into it.

He made himself concentrate as Inspector Carter replied, "That's more than I can say at present. It might have been a case of 'Did she fall or was she pushed?'"

"It could have been accidental?"

"That's what I said. On the other hand, if it was accidental, why was she buried in your College garden?"

Gawaine could think of more than one possible reply to that, but all he said, automatically, was, "Not my College."

"No?"

"Not any more."

Carter gave him that long, calculating look again, then shrugged. Desperately trying to be more efficient – not a state he normally pursued – Gawaine continued, "You're sure about the time she was put there? Thirty years ago?"

"So forensics tells me. Give or take a year. I gather it's

all to do with the decomposition of the small bones…they vanish in a particular order."

Gawaine really did not want to think about that. He was prepared to take Carter's word for it. "Have you any idea who she was?" he asked.

"No. In fact, from what we know so far, it looks as though someone – presumably whoever put her there – tried to obliterate anything that might have identified her. No handbag or purse, and what woman goes anywhere without them? Not enough left of her clothing to be much help. And we can confirm no wedding ring."

"But she was pregnant?"

"About six months."

Gawaine considered that. His own experience of pregnant women was practically non-existent, and he did not feel that an Oxford College, even if it was now co-residential, was the ideal place to extend it. Still, there was a point there somewhere that he would have to satisfy himself about. Perhaps David… But then, he reminded himself, his friend's experience of pregnant women was probably just as limited, though maybe for different reasons.

"Her teeth were in fairly good condition."

Gawaine forced himself away from speculation. "Any chance there – of identifying her, I mean?"

Carter shook his head. "She must be on someone's dental records, but where do you start looking? We're trying the local practices, but she doesn't have to be local. If we could track down her dentist we probably wouldn't need to, if you follow me." He shuffled a couple of pieces of paper in the file. "We can get a DNA sample," he went on, "but we haven't anything to compare it with. And if we can get a viable sample from the foetus, it might help us identify the father – but forensics isn't hopeful. Between the natural decaying of the DNA and the mess the workmen made when they first came across her..." He shrugged.

Gawaine's brain started whirling at the mention of DNA. "It might confirm something," he suggested tentatively, hoping he didn't sound too stupid.

"Find me something to confirm first." Carter grinned suddenly, seeming to unbend, and becoming rapidly more human. "Heck, she could be anybody. We're following up local missing persons reports for the right period, but I don't hold out much hope. As I said, she doesn't have to be local. She might have been a student, or come from somewhere else altogether. And her disappearance needn't have been reported in the first place." He gulped the rest of his coffee. "We've got the needle. We just don't know what haystack to plant it in."

That seemed to Gawaine a good note on which to leave. He felt more optimistic. The interview had not been too bad; he had not made any notable – or noticeable – blunders. Detective Inspectors who read John Donne, and who appeared to have the rudiments of a sense of humour, he found easier to deal with than those who persisted in treating him as if he were the sufferer from some rare but highly contagious disease. And the plant, after all, looked fairly healthy. Daringly Gawaine hummed a phrase or two of Vivaldi as he went to meet David.

David was heading for the Mitre where he was to meet Gawaine when he spotted a whole group of men and women, some of them carrying cameras, and dressed in the usual shabby denim and nylon anoraks. He suppressed a sigh. He supposed that it had only been a matter of time before the Press turned up.

Then David noticed that one of the crowd was snappy in pinstripes and patent leather. No one could mistake her glossy head, like a nicely polished horse chestnut. A very attractive view, but for once David would not have cared if he never got any closer.

"Shit," he hissed. There was no convenient corner to duck around, and a moment later the woman in question was standing in front of him, her eyes wide and a smile curling the corners of her mouth.

"Well, if it isn't the lovely Seff," David said.

"My friends call me Seff," Persephone Brown informed him coldly, the smile vanishing. "Ms Brown to you. Where's Gawaine?"

"Gawaine?" David echoed, bluffing frantically. "What about him?"

Seff tapped an irritable foot. "Come off it, David. Every time I've seen you out of a two-mile radius of the City, you've been with Gawaine. And we have a mysterious collection of bones discovered in the grounds of his former College. So where is he?"

"He's not talking to the Press."

"He'll talk to me."

The trouble was, David thought, he probably would. Gawaine loathed publicity, but he actually seemed to like Seff. And to do her justice, she was as honest and restrained as you could reasonably expect a reporter to be. David reluctantly admitted – purely to himself – that she was damn' good at her job.

"If I've got anything to do with it, you won't get within a mile of Gawaine," he said.

"Just try me. That sad lot – " Seff cocked her head at her esteemed colleagues, who were streaming along the street in the direction of the police station – "are on the way to a Press conference with whatshisname…Carter. And I'll have to join them. But now I know where it's at." Suddenly she gave David a brilliant smile. "You'll be seeing me again, David."

"I can't wait," David muttered as Seff turned away and headed after the rest of the group with a spring in her step. All he could hope was that Gawaine wouldn't encounter Seff as he left the police station.

To David's relief, when Gawaine arrived at the Mitre he appeared relatively calm, which suggested that the interview with Inspector Carter had gone well, and that Seff, so far, was not on his radar. David considered telling him that she was in Oxford, but decided that could wait.

"So what did Carter have to say?" he asked.

Over beer and sandwiches, Gawaine brought him up to date with what he had learnt. "Six months pregnant," he mused. "You know, that's nagging at me. How soon does a woman know she's pregnant?"

David shrugged. "Eight, ten weeks. She would probably suspect something sooner. And by six months, everyone who set eyes on her would know about it."

Gawaine gazed at him, wide-eyed. "My dear David, you're remarkably knowledgeable."

"Married sister," David explained.

"Really? Don't tell me you've got lots of little nephews and nieces?"

"One. Niece. And to get back to brass tacks – "

"To get back to brass tacks, six months is a bit late for her to come looking for her lover, demanding he make an honest woman of her."

"Hang on a minute," David said. "Aren't we making an assumption here? Even thirty years ago, she could have got an abortion if the baby was a problem."

Gawaine blinked. "Not everyone has quite such a cavalier attitude to problems," he murmured, then added more decisively, "Besides, if that was an option, she wouldn't have let the pregnancy go to six months, surely?"

David agreed, finishing his beer. "Do you want another of those?"

"No, thank you," Gawaine replied. "I get the feeling that I'm going to need a clear head for this next bit. Besides, since we're in Oxford, we may as well reserve getting drunk for the College claret." He frowned into the dregs at the bottom of his glass. "Where was I?"

"Six months pregnant."

"Mmm? Oh… Yes, suppose he was paying her, and then for some reason he stopped paying her. Might she not come and dump her little bundle – her potential little bundle, that is – on his doorstep?"

"But why would he stop paying?"

"Exactly. With your customary perspicacity, my dear David, you have hit the nail on the head. He would have to be pretty stupid to risk her coming to College to make a fuss, if he then felt obliged to kill her once she was there."

"If he was an undergraduate, he might not have had the money to go on paying her."

Gawaine considered this. "I don't think he was an

undergraduate. Oh, I've no doubt that undergraduates frequently get girls pregnant, but they surely don't murder them? They throw themselves on the mercy of their parents, or their moral tutors. I don't think they would be sent down for it, even thirty years ago. Whereas a don has more to lose. Reputation. Respectability. I think it was a don."

"And do you think you could put a name to the don?"

As soon as David said this, he regretted it. He had been enjoying the airy absurdity of Gawaine's approach to the problem, feeling it was much closer to his normal state of mind. Suddenly his friend's amusement vanished. He pushed away the remains of his lunch with a nervous gesture. "Templeman?" he asked sharply.

Having committed himself, there was nothing David could do but go on. "He's missing, isn't he? Or he was, yesterday."

"He is missing. You don't know this, David, but I had a word with Verner before I left. Templeman hasn't been seen since yesterday morning, and his bed wasn't slept in last night.

"Then he has done a bunk."

"He appears to have, as you say, done a bunk."

"As soon as the bones came to light."

Gawaine shook his head emphatically. "No!"

"What's the matter?"

"Templeman isn't…isn't like that. He really has – honesty, integrity, call it what you like. Goodness, if you want to be appallingly old-fashioned. If he wanted a girl I strongly suspect he would have married her first. He would certainly have married her afterwards."

"If he wasn't married already."

"No. As far as I know, he's never been married."

"Then perhaps she was a wild oat."

By now Gawaine was looking considerably upset. "But David, that's what I'm trying to tell you. If she had been, he would have taken the consequences. Married her, or whatever she wanted. That's what he was like. He wouldn't have killed her."

"All right. Take it easy. He has vanished, you know. You can't get round that."

"I know. But there'll be some explanation. Let's be getting back. I want to see the Dean."

David followed him out of the pub, annoyed with himself now for ever mentioning Templeman. Catching Gawaine up, he asked, "Did you know him well?"

"Who?"

"Templeman."

"I sat at his feet."

The answer was tossed off, superficial, irritating David until he saw how miserable Gawaine still looked. After a short silence he added slowly, "I owe him a lot."

He said nothing to explain that, and David did not feel he had any right to ask questions.

Chapter Five

'To be ignorant of evils to come, and forgetfull of evils past, is a mercifull provision in nature.'
Urne-Buriall, Ch 5

David followed Gawaine back to St Clement's in a state of rising bad temper. His friend had practically promised to extricate himself and leave, once he had spoken to the police, but somewhere along the way that promise had been forgotten. The reason was obvious. Templeman. David cursed him mentally with all the imagination of which an up-and-coming advertising executive is capable. He was well aware that until the problem of Templeman's disappearance was solved there would be no hope of removing Gawaine from Oxford.

Entering the college, Gawaine paused in the porter's lodge. Heatherington was on duty, staring at his mobile phone; David caught a glimpse of a football pool on the screen. Somewhere in the background a kettle was starting to sing. Heatherington was dug in very comfortably, David thought.

"Afternoon, sir," Heatherington said.

"Heatherington," Gawaine said, "when did you last see Dr Templeman?"

The porter grinned, relishing the question and the implications behind it. David suddenly realised that there was something subtly nasty about Heatherington. It crossed his mind to ask Gawaine if he knew where the porter had been thirty years ago.

"Ah, you'll be trying to track him down, sir," Heatherington said. He paused, but when Gawaine ignored the hint and offered no further explanation, he went on, "Well, now, it would be yesterday morning. He came for his post."

He gestured towards the opposite side of the lodge, to the set of pigeonholes fixed to the wall; a few of them held letters and packages.

"And was there any?" Gawaine asked.

"Two, sir. A letter – Bristol postmark, that would be from his sister, she writes every week – and a packet."

"What sort of a packet?"

Heatherington's hands traced an A4 shape in the air. "'Bout so big. Brown envelope. Could have been a journal. A very learned man, Dr Templeman."

"Quite. Did he say anything to you?"

"Only to pass the time of day, sir. A very friendly gentleman, always has a word for me, sir."

Gawaine nodded. "And then – when he'd finished passing the time of day – where did he go? Out? Or back into College?"

Heatherington's grin returned. "Back in, sir. And that's the last time I saw him. He didn't scarper, leastways, not when I was here." He gave that time to sink in before adding, "Young Simpson was on duty later on, sir. You could speak to him if you come in about six."

Gawaine murmured something non-committal and thanked him for his co-operation.

"Any time, sir. Any time." He peered at the phone screen again. "What do you reckon about Arsenal versus United?"

Gawaine had no opinion about Arsenal versus United; David strongly suspected that he had no idea what Heatherington was talking about.

He followed his friend as he drifted through the lodge and into the college grounds, where he was almost obliterated by a vigorous-looking man on his way out. The three-piece tweed ensemble he was wearing sat oddly on his athletic frame; David thought he would have looked more comfortable jogging in a track suit.

"Sorry," the man said, and added genially, "You must be St Clair?"

Gawaine admitted it.

"Colonel Morrison," the man introduced himself with a firm handshake. "Bursar. Rotten business this. Hope you get to the bottom of it."

He nodded in friendly fashion to David and went his way, leaving the impression of a small but resolute cyclone. David found it impossible to imagine him laid low by a stomach upset, or anything short of the Black Death.

"At least he seems to have reported for duty," Gawaine remarked. "I wish I could say the same of Templeman."

He went on, but instead of making for the main entrance to the College, he veered off into the gardens and along a path where a mass of delphiniums were preparing, in spectacular fashion, to do their seasonal thing, spires of blue flowers blazing out against the grey wall behind.

"Where are we going?" David asked.

Gawaine gave an airy gesture. "The Delphinium Walk, my dear David. The pride of the College gardeners. Also the prelude to – that."

Looking ahead, David could see that a section of the garden had been cordoned off; beyond the tapes, guarded by a solid and determined police constable, was an enclosure of canvas stretched on poles.

"That's where they found her?" David asked.

"As you say."

"They won't let you in."

"My dear David, I have not the slightest desire to be let in." He shuddered theatrically. "Would I be so ghoulish as to wish to contemplate for one moment – " He dropped onto a nearby bench. "Though the sight, from a distance, might stimulate the process of thought. What did you make of Heatherington?"

David sat on the bench beside him. "Nasty piece of work," he commented.

"Not my favourite person," Gawaine agreed. "But he started off an interesting train of thought."

"Yes?"

"What he told us must have been a very late sighting of Templeman – perhaps the latest, before he left College."

"But Heatherington said he didn't leave."

"Not then. He must have left later. Through the lodge, or one of the other gates. This is an establishment of learning, my dear David, not one of Her Majesty's prisons, and there are other ways in and out beside the porter's lodge. No, what I meant was the fact that he collected his post. He might have had news of something that meant he had to leave. Perhaps he never heard about – " he gestured up the garden towards the enclosure – "that, at all."

David considered. It was an attractive theory – at least, he could see why Gawaine might find it attractive. "Would he do that?" he asked. Go just like that? Wouldn't he have to sign out?"

Gawaine sighed; he could see the flaw in the theory. "Yes, of course he would. Or not exactly, but inform the Dean. And even if he had to dash – say, for a train – he's had over twenty-four hours to phone and explain."

He sighed again, sounding very tired, and then suddenly sat upright, alert once more. "If he left his post behind…" He stood up. "I wonder if the Dean…"

He was already making purposefully for the nearest door. Resignedly, David followed.

Stephen Verner had not been too pleased to hand over the key to Templeman's rooms, but when Gawaine explained about the post, he gave in.

"I brought you here," he muttered, scratching at his haystack of white hair. "I'd best co-operate. But I'll come with you. All above-board, then." As if he realised belatedly that someone less unassuming than Gawaine might have found that highly offensive, he added hastily, "There are those who think you shouldn't be here. I'll not give them cause for complaint."

Porteus, David thought silently, as he followed Gawaine and the Dean. *And others, most likely*. Not everyone in College would welcome a separate investigation. The thought would have discouraged him, but he could not repress a stir of excitement as they came to a halt outside a massive oak door on a landing in one of the oldest parts of the college. At last they might learn something. He half expected to see Templeman's dead body as Verner swung the door open, until he remembered that the Dean must have checked these rooms already, to make sure that the absent don really was absent.

To David, whose experience of dons' studies started and ended with Verner's, this room seemed unusually tidy. All the books were shelved, their cases covering two sides of the room. The large desk in front of the window was almost clear. There was an empty fireplace; on the mantelpiece was a large, ugly classical bust, which Gawaine addressed deferentially but incomprehensibly, provoking a snort of amusement from Verner.

"You've not forgotten your Greek."

Gawaine was already bending over the desk. Apart from pens in a tray, and a large leather-covered desk diary, the only object on it was a brown A4 envelope. Delicately Gawaine picked it up. It had been slit open; he peered inside.

"Reprints," he said disconsolately.

"What?" David asked.

"Reprints, my dear David. Copies of a paper he had published. On..." he peered again. "...ancient Roman antiquities. As one might expect. Nothing at all there to make him fly the coop."

"What about the letter?"

Gawaine glanced around and then crouched down to fossick about in the wastepaper basket. After a moment he straightened up.

"To coin a phrase," he remarked, "Eureka." He held a crumpled envelope. "Saturday's postmark, Bristol," he pointed out. "No letter in it, though." Turning to the Dean, he added, "I think you should phone Templeman's sister. He may have gone there."

"Without telling anyone?" Verner grunted disbelievingly.

"It's possible. Say she was seriously ill…"

It was evident even to David that if Templeman's sister was ill enough to drag him from Oxford in such a hurry that he left no trace of his passing, she would not have been posting a letter to tell him all about it on Saturday morning. *Emergencies*, he thought, *get announced by phone or email.* But it was quite obvious that Gawaine was ignoring for as long as possible the much less pleasant alternative, so he said nothing.

Meanwhile, Gawaine had flicked open the desk diary and found the current page. "Interesting…" he murmured, pointing to an entry for the previous day. Beside the space for 1.00pm it read: Lunch – M.

"M?" Gawaine asked, with an inquiring look at Verner.

The Dean shrugged. "Could be Morrison. He and Templeman are good friends. They play chess together."

Gawaine frowned slightly, as if the answer didn't please him. "Morrison didn't make it to lunch yesterday," he said thoughtfully. Remember, he had a stomach upset."

Seeming to dismiss the detail, he crossed the study and opened the door of the bedroom. "Mmm…" he murmured.

He looked worried. Joining him, David could see why. On the bed was a neatly folded pair of pyjamas, and on the bedside table a paperback novel with a bookmark in it, a glasses case and a mobile phone plugged into its charger.

Before he could speak, Gawaine darted away again, to another door which led to a bathroom.

"Shaving things and a toothbrush," he said, a brittle note in his voice.

"Looks as if he went in a hurry," Verner remarked.

Gawaine took a breath as if about to say something else, but he remained silent, only giving a sharp shake of the head. He had gone quite white.

David, not understanding, went over to him. "Let's get out of here."

Gawaine looked up at him with a faint smile." Oh, yes, by all means. In these cases, you shouldn't disturb anything, should you?" He put a warning hand on David's arm, silencing anything he might have said, and turned to Verner. "He may have kept the traditional bag of necessaries ready for an abrupt departure." By now David could tell that he didn't believe a word of it. "There doesn't seem to be a suitcase here."

"It would be in the trunk room," Verner explained. "We can go and look, if you like."

Gawaine nodded. He seemed to relax slightly when they left Templeman's rooms, but David, who had seen him all too often gripped by a fit of the horrors, knew perfectly well that this one was not over yet. And he thought that if he had a few minutes to consider it, he might well be able to work out why.

They were approaching the next landing on the way down the stairs when a door flew open.

"What the hell is going on?"

It was Porteus. He looked furious, which David reflected might be his normal state. He was obviously poised for battle, though slightly taken aback when he saw Verner.

"Oh, it's you, Dean," he said, and added with a bad grace, "Sorry. But I heard noises upstairs in Templeman's rooms – "

"Just a small point that had to be checked," the Dean rumbled pleasantly. "Nothing to worry about."

Porteus stood in his open doorway, glancing sharply from Verner to Gawaine and back again. Behind him was a desk spread with papers; he must have been disturbed, David thought, at the sharp end of scholarly endeavour.

Beside him, David felt Gawaine stiffen. He was not sure what had caused that reaction: not dislike of his ex-tutor, for he had not reacted when Porteus first appeared.

"When did you last see Dr Templeman?" Gawaine inquired.

"None of your damn' business," Porteus snapped.

Verner stepped forward. "All the same..." he began.

Porteus's head swivelled towards him. "Sunday night at dinner, if you must know."

Probably no one but David heard Gawaine's sharp intake of breath; he was thrilling with tension. "You didn't see him yesterday morning at all?" he asked.

By this time Porteus was managing to get his temper under some control, but there was poison in his voice as he replied. "I was under the impression that is what I just said." Gawaine inclined his head in acknowledgement. "And now, if you have no objection, I'd rather like to get on with some work."

He slammed the door shut.

Verner shook his head regretfully. "Touchy, very touchy." He went on past Porteus's door, then paused to add, "A brilliant mind, but touchy."

They followed him down the stairs.

"Are you all right?" David muttered.

Gawaine glanced up at him. His dreamy blue eyes were brilliant, too vivid in his paper-white face. "No," he replied, and there was something in his voice, a scarcely audible whisper, that terrified David. "I am of the opinion that something remarkably nasty is about to manifest itself. I should prefer not to be here when it does, but unfortunately I have not left myself that option."

That was something David could understand, though he did not agree. In the last few minutes – since they had searched Templeman's rooms – Gawaine's reactions had altered radically, and all David's instincts were to get him away from there.

"Now, look – " he began.

Gawaine shook his head. Following Verner, they were on ground level again, and Verner had come to a halt in front of another massive door. "Trunk room is down here," he explained as he fumbled with the bunch of keys. "Part of the cellar. Too damp for wine, but just right for growing mould on leather."

He found the right key, turned it, and pulled at the door. It yielded, creaking. Gawaine stepped forward, feeling for a light switch. Finding it, he switched on.

David saw him step back, and say in an odd, quiet voice, "No."

He switched the light off again, but not before David had seen, over his shoulder, stone stairs leading down, and at the bottom a tumble of limbs, the head at a grotesque angle, the staring eyes. David had never seen Templeman, but he had no doubt that the missing don was no longer missing.

Chapter Six

'Every man is his own Atropos, and lends a hand to cut the thread of his own days.'

Religio Medici

About ten minutes – or a couple of centuries, however you looked at it – later, Gawaine was lying on the bed in his own room. His eyes were closed and he was shivering. David, who had put him there, wished he could have fainted and have done with it. He himself was looking out of the window, trying hard not to think about that disorderly huddle of limbs, so vividly revealed at the foot of the stairs, when Gawaine stirred and spoke.

"If only I'd started thinking a bit earlier."

David turned to face him. "Rubbish!" he said caustically. "You know perfectly well he was dead before we got here."

"I don't know that."

"It's – "

A tap on the outer door interrupted what David was saying. He went through to answer it; the door opened to reveal Verner, carrying a tray with a decanter of whisky and two glasses.

"Thought you might be in need of that," he said. "I've just been on to the police. They're on their way." His gaze went past David to the open bedroom door. "How's St Clair?"

"Not good."

"Doctor?"

David considered. He was aware that Gawaine was in shock, and that a mild sedative would do no harm at all, but he was also aware of Gawaine's terror of anything with an MD attached to it.

"No," he said. "He'll be okay."

"Feed him some of that," Verner advised, thrusting the tray at him. "I've got to go and meet the police. They'll be wanting to talk to the two of you, I expect."

"Then they can bloody well wait!" David said; the Dean, departing, made no reply. David went back into the bedroom.

Gawaine looked up as he appeared. "Was that Verner?" he asked in a colourless voice.

"Yes. The police are on their way."

David put the tray down on the bedside table and poured drinks, though Gawaine only shook his head at the glass that was offered to him.

"He was a very devious croquet player," he observed.

"Verner?"

"Templeman."

David wondered what that had to do with anything, but wisely did not ask. He went to the washbasin and dripped water into his whisky, not because he wanted it, but because something Puritanical in him objected to neat whisky in the middle of the afternoon.

Gawaine watched as he drank, and asked, "Is it any good?"

David had not really been thinking beyond the need for a stiff drink. "Not bad," he reported. "Single malt. Glenfiddich," he added, a step in the dark.

Gawaine bent over his own glass, sniffed, and sipped. "Laphroaig. You have a frightful palate, David. Mind you," he went on fretfully, "in my present state it could be Red Biddy and I shouldn't be capable of telling the difference." The glass beat a faint staccato on the tray as he put it down again.

"Take it easy," David said. "When we've spoken to the police, we can go."

"Go!" Gawaine sat up abruptly. "My dear David, even if the police let us go, which I consider highly unlikely, do you really think that we can extricate ourselves now?" He paused and then said more hesitantly, "At least, you – "

"Forget about that. Why not? You've spoken to the police, they can't identify the girl, and now you've found Templeman. Isn't that enough?"

Gawaine shook his head. He was recovering, David thought; at least, his present agitation was a step in the right direction. He leant back against the pillows and absent-mindedly swallowed the whisky David had poured for him.

"Listen, David. Remember what I said to Verner. They dug her up in the college gardens and there was no evidence at all to show who put her there. Nothing." He took a breath and passed a hand across his face; David could sense the effort that was going into his self-control. "But now there's Templeman. Lying at the bottom of the trunk room stairs with a broken neck. A broken neck, David."

David thought the self-control was about to snap. He crossed to the table and replenished their glasses.

Gawaine gave him a helpless, apologetic look. "Drunk, I should be a perfectly appalling mess."

With a renewed effort, he took a deep breath and was able to continue, rapidly, impersonally, as if what had happened had nothing to do with him. "Yesterday morning, Templeman heard what they found in the garden. And it meant something to him. If he didn't know who she was, he knew she was connected with someone in College. So he went to talk to – someone. Who killed him by pushing him down the trunk room stairs. It isn't true any longer, what I said to Verner. The murderer hasn't left the College. He's still here, David, and he's committed two murders. One thirty years ago, and one yesterday."

He was shivering again by the time he had finished. David found that, unaccountably, he had finished the second glass of whisky. He sat down at the end of the bed, well away from the temptation of the third, and asked, without much hope, "Are you sure? Templeman might have fallen."

"And who locked the door? We saw Verner unlock it ourselves. That's something we shall need to check. Who has a key to the trunk room? Not everyone, surely?"

David nodded. An even nastier idea was forming in his mind. "So if Templeman was killed because he knew," he began slowly, "and he was going to tell what he knew, then the murderer is prepared to kill to keep things quiet. And you…"

"And I had better not stand at the head of the stairs in the company of anyone I cannot trust." Gawaine finished his sentence in light, brittle tones that effectively hid what he was really feeling.

"Don't tell me it doesn't bother you," David said sombrely.

"Of course it bothers me. It terrifies me." Gawaine managed a quick smile, that somehow made it all the clearer he meant what he said.

"Then why stay?"

"Sheer bloody-mindedness, my dear David."

That was no answer at all, but David refrained from pointing this out. He knew Gawaine, he had seen him frightened before, and still not letting that get in the way of what he thought he had to do. For sheer, pig-headed obstinacy, he was hard to beat. And there was something about St Clement's College, or about Gawaine's attitude to it, David thought, that he hadn't caught on to yet. There would be even less point than usual in trying to make him pack up and go home – paradoxically, because he really didn't want to be there.

"So what happens now?" he asked, resigned again to the inevitable.

Rather unsteadily, Gawaine got to his feet and reached for the tie he had discarded when he lay down.

"Are you sure you're all right?" David asked.

"Really, my dear David, a fit of the vapours is a luxury I can't afford at the moment. I must speak to the police. I need to know who was the last person to see Templeman yesterday. So far he vanishes from human ken when he left the lodge with his post."

"I suppose the last person to see him was his murderer," David contributed.

"True, but there must have been at least one other."

"Why?"

Gawaine peered at him, and then seemed to decide that there was a functional brain concealed somewhere, in spite of evidence to the contrary. "Because, my dear David," he explained patiently, "someone must have told him about the bones."

"Oh – I see."

David turned that over in his mind while Gawaine put on his shoes and went to brush his hair in the same inadequate mirror. Eventually he asked, "Do you think this woman was connected with Templeman, then?"

Gawaine murmured something that might have been, "Heaven preserve us!" before turning to him. "No, I do not. If she was, we can assume he would have made some attempt to find her, thirty years ago. But he knew there was, or had been, a woman. And then there was no longer a woman. And he accepted someone's explanation of where she went. But yesterday, faced with a body in the college gardens, he suddenly realised what really happened to her, and he went to talk to her murderer. His murderer."

"That was stupid."

"That was Templeman. Not stupid, just very, very straight-forward. He would never condemn anyone without hearing their side of the story first. And he wouldn't have told anyone else until he heard it. Whereupon his murderer – "

"Call him X."

"Call him…no, David. All murderers are called X. Let us at least be original. Call him…M."

"M for murderer?" David asked. "Or M for whoever it was that Templeman was going to meet for lunch?"

Gawaine gave him a critical look and a nod that seemed to readmit him to the company of *homo sapiens*. "That does indeed bear thinking about. It might have been Morrison, but I doubt it. If you meet someone most days for lunch on High Table, do you bother writing it down in your diary?"

"Then that suggests his murderer doesn't belong in College at all. Either Templeman went out of College to meet him – "

"Which we know he didn't, because we found his body here."

"Or M came here. In which case we ought to be looking for someone from outside."

Gawaine shrugged. "People come and go all the time. How are you going to identify Templeman's guest, now that Templeman is dead? Besides, we know that the murderer is here, in St Clement's."

"Okay," David conceded. "Then you might call him P, or H."

"Porteus or Heatherington? You may speak wiser than you know, my dear David. Did you notice – "

He broke off at a knock on the outer door, and went to answer it. David followed him, still not convinced that he was fit to carry on. At the door was the Dean.

"St Clair? I've got the police in my room."

"Accept my condolences," Gawaine murmured.

"Glad to see you're on your feet again," Verner went on. "Can you come and talk now?"

"Delighted. Except that before we go, can you tell me who has access to the trunk room?"

Verner scratched his head, making his hair even more untidy. "Keys?" He gave it a moment's thought. "I have a complete set myself. So does the Master. And there's a set hanging on a board in the porter's lodge."

"Heatherington," David said with a certain amount of satisfaction.

"Yes, but..." The Dean looked suddenly disconcerted. He seemed to have realised that what he was giving was a list of suspects. "That doesn't tell you anything," he went on. "Anyone who wanted a particular key could go and ask for it at the lodge. I can see that a murderer wouldn't ask, but if the porter wasn't there, he could just take it. And if he put it back afterwards, no one would ever know."

Gawaine nodded slowly. "I must ask Heatherington about that," he said. "Though if he is involved he will most certainly lie." He sighed deeply. "Frightfully confusing."

He fell silent, thinking, and after a brief pause the Dean prompted him, "The police?"

"I'm sorry. Of course." He gave a quick glance at David. "Excuse me. See you later."

He disappeared through the door and down the stairs. David moved to follow him. "Hang on! What did you mean just now, did I notice?"

No answer came back.

Chapter Seven

'What song the Sirens sang, or what name Achilles assumed when he hid himself among women, though puzzling questions, are not beyond all conjecture.'

Urne-Buriall, Ch 5

David did not see Gawaine again until that evening. He had his own, singularly unproductive, interview with the police, and emerged into a college where anyone he might conceivably have spoken to had vanished in pursuit of learning, sleep, or beer.

Since he was technically working from home, he retired to his room and spent a couple of hours communing with his laptop and the contracts for which he was responsible. But these delights failed to hold his attention. As time passed, he became increasingly disturbed that Gawaine hadn't reappeared, especially in a college with an unidentified murderer lurking about. Eventually, David saved his work and headed out to look for him.

After a while he found his way into the college gardens, where he wandered for a while, noting without much interest a fishpond with a statue that attested to the classical broad-mindedness of those who harboured it, a sundial that was half an hour slow, and a piece of modern sculpture which reminded him of a certain well-known brand of mint. He ended his peregrinations in the Delphinium Walk, within sight of the sinister canvas enclosure, where he found Gawaine seated on a bench with sketch pad and pencil; he was drawing a particularly ugly gargoyle that protruded from the college roof.

"Where do you think you've been?" David asked sourly.

Gawaine replied as if the answer should have been obvious. "Lining up suspects."

"Oh?"

Gawaine indicated the free end of the seat he was occupying, and David sat down. "So what have you been up to?" he asked.

"I tracked Heatherington to his lair," Gawaine explained. "His local, that is – a perfectly frightful little pot-house, and the beer makes one lose the will to live. But we did have a very interesting conversation about this and that, notably who was here thirty years ago, and is still here."

This sounded promising to David, who began to sit up and take notice. "Who?" he asked.

"Heatherington himself, for one. Though I couldn't make too much of that, obviously. He wasn't head porter then, and I don't suppose he would have lost his job if his sins had come home to roost. But he was married – at least, he has a son about my age, so I assume he was married."

"So a spare girl turning up would have been a nuisance."

"Exactly – though whether she would have been sufficient nuisance to be worth murdering… However, he's on the list."

Abstractedly he watched a bee doing its duty by the delphiniums, until recalled by an impatient noise from David. “Sorry – where was I?”

“What did Heatherington tell you?”

“Quite a lot, but what it boils down to is that there are four other suspects. Father Gerard, Porteus, the Bursar and the Dean.”

“The Dean?” David repeated in surprise. “That can’t be right. Why would he have brought you here, if he did it?”

Gawaine gave him an affectionate look. “My dear David, you have a high opinion of my abilities. Perhaps Verner doesn’t share it. Goodness knows, he has no reason to.”

“But to bring you here – and plenty of people didn’t approve of that – it’s a bit unnecessary, isn’t it?”

Gawaine shrugged elegantly. “Maybe. But it would divert suspicion, too. That’s an old trick.”

“But he phoned you – that must have been just after Templeman...”

As if he liked it, Gawaine repeated the shrug. “That doesn’t mean to say he didn’t do it.”

David tried to weigh up Gawaine, wondered if the streak of cynicism was genuine, came to no conclusion, and tried a shrug of his own, less successfully. “What was the Dean’s motive?” he asked.

“Well, we know the motive for killing Templeman, the same in every case: because he knew too much. It’s the murder of the girl that we need to look at. Now, according to Heatherington, thirty years ago Verner was engaged to be married.”

"A bit late," David remarked, thinking of the present age of the Dean.

"Not excessively. At any rate, so he was, to a lady, for our purposes, of very considerable interest."

"Oh?"

Gawaine favoured him with a cat-like smile. "A bishop's daughter, my dear David, with, to quote Heatherington, 'a tidy bit of her own.'"

David began to understand why Gawaine was giving so much attention to the Dean. "A rich wife…" he murmured.

"And a bishop's daughter. And, most significant of all, not quite his wife. Bishops' daughters, like Caesar's wife, have to be above suspicion. And so do bishops' daughters' husbands." He paused, as if checking mentally that he had got that right, and went on, "She wouldn't be inclined to sweep his little peccadillo under the carpet, and he wouldn't want to marry this other, less socially desirable girl instead. A perfect motive."

"Do you think he did it?" David asked.

At the direct question, Gawaine's satisfaction evaporated. "I don't want to," he said. I rather like Verner – when he isn't putting the fear of God into me. And I've always thought of him as honest. He – "

"You don't want to think anyone did it," David interrupted. "You were fussing at lunch time because you thought it might have been Templeman."

Gawaine acknowledged the truth of that with a faint sigh.

"So what about the others?" David continued. "The Bursar, or Porteus, or Father…Thing."

"Gerard. The chaplain. Even less likely, I should say."

"But he was here?"

"Yes."

"Then what about him?" David insisted. "I don't suppose college chaplains are any more moral than the rest of us."

"I rather hope they are," Gawaine murmured.

He looked all set for a diversion into comparative ethics, and David, forestalling it hastily, asked, "Is he married?"

"No. He's an Anglo-Catholic, and deliberately celibate."

"Rather him than me."

Gawaine cleared his throat. "Quite. However, my dear David, he has remained within the Anglican communion, and so in the – what I can only describe as the unlikely event of his getting a girl pregnant in the first place – in that case, there would be nothing actually to prevent his marrying her."

"If he wanted to."

"Of course, he would no longer have been able to remain a celibate priest. Although if he had gone so far as to sleep with a girl in the first place, he might have been led to question his vocation. In any case, murdering her looks a bit drastic, doesn't it?"

David nodded. He was remembering his encounter with Father Gerard at High Table the night before. The chaplain, ascetic, saintly, and yet surprisingly all there, did not fit the conventional idea of a murderer. And his motive was nothing like as good as Verner's.

"What about the Bursar?" David asked.

"Colonel Morrison? I don't think he sounds likely. He's rather younger than the others, and thirty years ago he was here as an undergraduate. If you remember, we thought it unlikely that it was an undergraduate."

"We could be wrong."

"Mmm..." Gawaine mused, eyes half closed. "Why not marry her, then? Also, my dear David," he went on more alertly, "he spent twenty-four years in the regular army. When his engagement ended, two years ago, he was offered the post of Bursar. Now I may be over-sensitive, but if I had buried a body, I should start sweeping the streets rather than take a job where I had to pass the spot every day."

David tried and failed to imagine Gawaine sweeping the streets. However, he took his point.

"And he wasn't here yesterday," Gawaine continued. "He had that stomach upset. Remember?"

"Now that's suspicious, to start with."

Gawaine looked amused. "Of course, my dear David, in a detective story, always suspect the man with an alibi. But his wife rang in, and that must have been before Templeman was killed...I suppose. I'll check with the Dean."

For all his doubts about the alibi, David could not help but admit that there seemed no particular reason for suspecting the Bursar. With a certain relief, he turned to the man who had been his own personal front runner all along. "Tell me about Porteus."

Instead of replying at once, Gawaine frowned and sat staring into the middle distance, but before David could prompt him, he came to himself with a little shiver. "Porteus – yes, of course."

"What about him?"

"Porteus is very interesting. He wasn't an undergraduate here, for one thing. He came here with his doctorate, from Manchester, I believe, as the Griffin Fellow."

"Good for him," David muttered.

"The Griffin Fellowship, my dear David – " Gawaine spoke didactically – "is a research award lasting for three years, traditionally given to a newly qualified doctor, and also traditionally leading to a permanent post within the College. It is therefore highly desirable, and given only to the best. It has one major condition attached to it: that the Fellow remain unmarried for the period of the Fellowship."

David grinned. "Ah."

"Well may you say, 'Ah'. Quite clearly, if Porteus was faced with this girl demanding marriage, he couldn't marry her without giving up one of the most coveted academic jobs in the country, and wrecking his future career as well. Assuming the girl wouldn't wait..."

"The child would have been out of nappies."

"Of course, my dear David, you know about these things. A niece, wasn't it? All the same," he added, shaking his head slightly, "surely any reasonable woman would have settled for a flat in Oxford and a wedding once Porteus's Fellowship was up? Three years isn't long to wait, especially with a good job at the end of it for her future husband."

"Then maybe she wasn't reasonable," David suggested. "Maybe she didn't trust him."

"Maybe," Gawaine agreed. "And Porteus, of course, coming from out of Oxford, had the best possible opportunity for sowing a wild oat or two unknown to the rest of the College." He hesitated, and then went on, "And there's something else I can tell you about Porteus."

"What?"

Gawaine got to his feet and brushed himself off. "Let's go and find somewhere to have dinner," he suggested. "I don't think I can face High Table tonight."

"Well, yes," David said, hurriedly following his friend along the path that led to the porter's lodge. "But, Gawaine – listen, damn it! What can you tell me about Porteus?"

Gawaine smiled at him serenely. "Do you remember, my dear David, that I asked you earlier if you noticed anything when we were talking to Porteus outside his rooms?"

"Yes."

"You did? What?"

They passed through the lodge. A younger man was on duty; Gawaine nodded to him but did not pause.

"Not yes I noticed," David said, exasperated. "Yes I remember."

Gawaine sighed. "This way. No, you don't need your car. Why do you think the good Lord gave you feet? Well – " forestalling by perhaps five seconds another murder – "when Porteus had his door open, I could see his desk."

"So could I. So what?"

"You didn't notice what was on the desk?"

"No. If Templeman had been stabbed, it might have been a blood-stained dagger. But as he was shoved down a flight of stairs – "

"Really, my dear David!" Gawaine interrupted. "Even if Templeman had been stabbed, would his murderer leave the weapon in full view? Not but what," he added soberly, "that it might not be a piece of evidence just as damning."

"What?"

"Nothing unusual. Just one of Templeman's reprints."

Chapter Eight

'Where I cannot satisfy my reason, I love to humour my fancy.'

Religio Medici

"Are you sure?" David asked.

It was two hours later. A highly satisfactory dinner was coming to an end with brandy.

"About Templeman's reprint?" Gawaine asked. "Positive."

"It couldn't have been a different reprint?"

"No. I looked at the packet in Templeman's rooms, remember. The front page of the article was nearly all taken up with a photograph of a very distinctive bit of statuary."

David recollected what he had seen in the middle of the fishpond. "Oh yes?"

"Not distinctive in that sense," Gawaine said severely. "Pick your mind up out of the gutter, my dear David. It was, however, undoubtedly the same photograph in the reprint on Porteus's desk. Now we know that Templeman picked up that set of reprints from the porter's lodge just after breakfast yesterday, which proves that he must have seen Porteus between then and the time he was killed."

"Doesn't prove Porteus killed him, though."

"No, but what is interesting is that he lied about it. When I saw the reprint, I made a particular point of asking him to confirm in so many words that he hadn't seen Templeman since dinner the night before. And in front of witnesses. That might be very useful."

Gawaine sipped brandy in silence for a few minutes before continuing. "We ought to trace what Templeman was doing that morning, and who was the last person to see him. And, for that matter, what all our suspects were doing as well. We know that Colonel Morrison was at home on his bed of pain. If any of the others have a rock solid alibi, then we can eliminate them as well."

"They won't like it," David commented. "Being questioned."

"No...perhaps I could persuade Inspector Carter to come clean."

"Trade information," David suggested. At Gawaine's inquiring look, he added, "About the reprint."

Gawaine considered, frowning. "I'm not too sure I like that. It hardly seems sporting, somehow."

David refrained from pointing out that it was not sport they were engaged in. Even though Gawaine had a total lack of interest in sport of any kind, he came from a long line of aristocrats who had swarmed across the playing fields of Eton and had never, under any circumstances, contemplated shooting a fox.

"It isn't as if you like Porteus," he said.

Gawaine gave him a bleak look. "That, my dear David, is why."

David let it go at that. As he had thought, it was the English gentleman's sense of fair play, which Gawaine suffered from in a highly advanced form. David found it admirable and extremely irritating, and felt profoundly thankful that he himself was not afflicted with it.

"More brandy?" he asked.

It would be an excellent idea, he thought, if he could return Gawaine to college, not drunk – he had never seen Gawaine drunk – but slightly euphoric, anaesthetised at least against the realities of the day. He was mildly surprised when Gawaine accepted, with a faint, apologetic smile, as if he was perfectly well aware of what David had in mind.

It was not until the second brandy had been brought that he announced, "Something is bothering me."

"What's that?" David asked, reflecting that there must be at least fifty things bothering him.

Gawaine slowly swirled the brandy and stared at the patterns on the glass. "If I were a betting man, my dear David, I should be prepared to stake a certain amount on the possibility that Templeman was not killed where we found him."

"Why not?"

"Because I can think of no reason why he should have visited the trunk room in the company of the man he suspected of having killed that girl."

David looked at that and considered it. "The police will know," he said.

"Exactly. And if they know where he was killed, that might provide a little enlightenment. And that leads me on to something else."

He fell silent. David waited, assuming what he hoped was an inviting expression.

"It would be highly unlikely," Gawaine went on at last, "that the police would have accepted Templeman's death as an accident, when the first body had just been found. Especially when she died in exactly the same way. M – the murderer, if you recall – M must have hidden the body in the first available place, intending to dispose of it more permanently later. However..." He paused, drank, and continued, "However, why did M bury the first body, the girl's body? Why not report that death as an accident?"

David had not thought about that before. "There must have been something," he said. "Marks of a struggle..."

"Oh, yes. There must be some explanation. I should like to know what it is, that's all. Suppose she did die accidentally. You don't go looking for trouble by burying the body – which must have been a very difficult thing to do, single-handed. And if she was murdered – well, if you can pass it off as accident, you've committed the perfect crime, so once again, why bury the body?" He shook his head, frowning. "There's something there, my dear David, that doesn't quite add up."

When they left the restaurant the night was clear and cool. To David's relief, Gawaine seemed quite relaxed – whether from the effects of good brandy or rational discussion was not clear. He said nothing about bodies, buried or otherwise, but was content to meander slowly back to college, falling gradually into a vein of reminiscence of earlier, and hairier, undergraduate days. David listened with half an ear.

"...putting *things*, my dear David, that is objects of a certain nature, on top of the Martyrs' Memorial. Now, that was never really up my street. Too fearfully athletic. The great days of climbing into college were already over, of course, though there were still certain accepted routes. But I was far too law-abiding."

"Naturally," David murmured.

Gawaine glanced at him as if suspecting sarcasm. "Virtue, or a healthy terror of Dr Verner..." he began, then broke off as David came to an abrupt halt. "Well?" he asked when no explanation was forthcoming.

They stood still at the foot of the aforesaid Martyrs' Memorial, at present unadorned by any items of undergraduate plumbing. David was struggling with a theory.

"All this..." he began. "Climbing around college roofs, lugging this that and the other..."

"The merry games of undergraduate existence," Gawaine supplied encouragingly. "Someone once put a Morris Minor on the chapel roof. What about it?"

"Why couldn't someone have brought the body into college like that? She didn't have to be killed there at all."

Gawaine stared at him. "Roof-climbing with a dead body?" He gave an affected shudder. "You show an unexpected taste for the macabre, my dear David."

"It's possible."

Gawaine shook his head slightly with a pained expression, and moved off again. David followed him into Broad Street.

"It's possible," he repeated. "For someone who wanted to get rid of a body. Bury her in someone else's college. Maybe not over the wall, but sneak her in through a gate. That would mean the murderer isn't necessarily connected with St Clement's at all."

Gawaine gave him a sidelong glance. "You may have a point. Impossible to check now which gates would have been locked, whether the porter on duty was keeping his eyes open, and so on and so on, thirty years ago. But then…who murdered Templeman?"

"M, who came in to have lunch with him?"

Gawaine considered that for all of two seconds, then shook his head. "Highly unlikely. There was no time for M to find out that the bones had been dug up, and then arrange to meet Templeman for lunch."

"But suppose Templeman did the inviting? Ready to ask a few awkward questions?"

This time, David was pleased to see, Gawaine looked more interested. "Possible," he conceded. "But I'm still not happy with the idea of sneaking the body into college. Why not drive it out into the country and dump it there?"

David had no answer to that. It was a pity, he thought. His theory had one outstanding attraction: it would have opened up the field of suspects once again to such an extent that there would have been nothing left for Gawaine to do.

With a mental groan, David relinquished the idea. They turned into Catte Street, walked down the High, and were approaching the lodge of St Clement's, when a figure emerged and crossed the pavement to the police car that was parked there.

Gawaine quickened his pace. "Inspector Carter."

The Inspector stopped with his hand on the door handle of the car. "Mr St Clair. What can I do for you?"

"Are there any developments, Inspector?" Inspector Carter hesitated; David wondered if he was going to answer. He looked discouraged. "I can't tell you who killed Dr

Templeman," he said at last. "But I suppose there are one or two things you ought to know. He died of a broken neck, though I don't imagine that will be news to you. There's nothing to show that he didn't just have a bad fall, except – "

"Except that someone subsequently pushed him down into the trunk room," Gawaine finished edgily.

Carter blinked, then gave Gawaine a long, thoughtful look. "You worked that out, did you? Yes, he was put there after death. It looks as if he died by falling down his own staircase."

"Or being pushed down it," Gawaine murmured. "Pity."

"Why?" David asked.

"Because where he was killed might have given us a pointer to who killed him. But if it was his own staircase, it doesn't help us much." He took the time for a thoughtful pause, then asked the Inspector," Do you know who was the last person to see Dr Templeman alive?"

"I think so. You know about the visit to the lodge, of course? He collected his mail, and at some point he must have gone back to his own rooms, because that packet of papers is there. But he was seen a bit later by one of your dons – a young chap called Birkett." Gawaine had no comment to make, and the Inspector carried on. "Birkett just happened to be going through the gardens at the time the workmen found the body. The foreman called him over, and Birkett went with him to report to the Dean. On his way, he met Dr Templeman and – being in a bit of a state as far as I can tell – told him what was going on. Templeman went out into the gardens, had a look for himself and a quick word with the workmen, and then went back into college. And that's the last time anyone admits to seeing him."

"Interesting," Gawaine remarked.

"It's interesting that the last people who spoke to him were the workmen, who can't possibly be involved in his murder."

Gawaine nodded slowly. Though he said nothing, David had the idea that was not what he thought interesting. It left a wide field of speculation as to what he had meant.

"I assume you saw the lunch date in Templeman's diary," Inspector Carter went on. "It's tempting, but I don't think there's anything for us there. I'd guess Templeman was killed long before one o'clock."

"Was Templeman carrying his post when Birkett met him?" Gawaine asked, not arguing with that.

"He thinks not."

That was an admirable opening for Gawaine to tell Carter about Porteus and the reprint, but he said nothing, merely thanking him and taking a graceful farewell.

David followed him through the lodge into college. "You didn't say anything about that reprint."

"No," Gawaine agreed equably.

"Does it occur to you that if Porteus is the man we're after, it's in your interest to have him dealt with before he deals with you?"

Gawaine gave him a guileless look. "Of course, my dear David. But if Templeman went back to his rooms before Birkett saw him – and he did, because he deposited his post there – then he had a chance to give Porteus the reprint quite innocently."

"Then why is Porteus lying about it?"

Gawaine shrugged. "There could be several reasons. And I think I should give him the chance to explain before I throw him to the hounds."

David thought it highly unlikely that Porteus would offer Gawaine an explanation, in view of his behaviour to date. Before he could say so, however, Gawaine spoke again.

"There is another fact that we might consider. Porteus and Templeman shared a staircase."

Chapter Nine

'Had not almost every man suffered by the Press, or were not the tyranny thereof become universal, I had not wanted reason for complaint.'

Religio Medici

The next morning, David found himself attending the inquest on the bones in St Clement's College garden. Gawaine was not there. After a prolonged discussion on the night before, followed by a pill to make him sleep, he had been no more than semi-conscious when David left.

David had no objection to standing in for him. In a few days they would both have to be present, to give evidence at the inquest on Richard Templeman. For the time being, Gawaine might as well rest.

Glad that he was not personally involved, David glanced round the court. He noticed without much enthusiasm that the Press were there in force; Seff was among them, and gave him a little wave when he caught her eye. Measuring the distance from his seat to the door, David hoped to leave before she could catch him, once the proceedings were over.

He was unfortunate. He might have managed to slip away if it hadn't been for a bottleneck at the exit, but as he was trying to negotiate the crowd he felt a pencil being poked into his ribs. He jerked and turned round.

"You again," he sighed.

"Me again," Seff agreed brightly. "Now, what about taking me to see Gawaine?"

"I already told you – "

"Come on, David," Seff interrupted, giving him another prod with the object that was not a pencil, but the stylus of her smartphone. "Give me a break."

"A break? The only break you need is in the neck."

David thought that was rather neat, but Seff was unimpressed.

"I've got a job to do." Suddenly she gave David a brilliant smile. "I'll treat him very gently, David. Kid gloves. Silk and velvet."

David was not convinced. But still…let her in, and they might avoid the worst of the others. Gawaine would have to go public later, at Templeman's inquest, and the mob of journalists that was just leaving would frighten the life out of him. If he told his story to Seff, he would be stale news by then.

Seff saw David's hesitation and rammed home her advantage. "Let me talk to him, and I'll let him vet the piece before I send it. Otherwise you can both take what comes."

Not long after, David was escorting Seff through the porter's lodge of St Clement's. None of the other reporters had so far made an appearance. Heatherington, on duty, gave David an evil wink as they passed through. Not much question about what was going through his mind. And there were times when David came close to regretting that Seff would never let him within a mile of her bed. He couldn't stand the woman, but she was exciting.

Now Gawaine, who got on well with her, never thought of her like that. At least, what Gawaine thought was his own business, but in his personal code you did not, when meeting an attractive woman, immediately start weighing up the advantages of taking her to bed. It was an attitude that David supposed had much to recommend it, though at the moment he couldn't quite think what.

His meditations took them to the bottom of Gawaine's staircase. "Wait here," he ordered Seff. "Soak up atmosphere or something."

Seff mutely raised her eyes to heaven. David made sure, as he went upstairs, that she was not following him.

Outside Gawaine's room, he hesitated. He was not having second thoughts – there was never any point, in dealing with Seff – but he was a bit worried about how to put it to Gawaine. Or if it came to that, about what sort of state Gawaine would be in. Awake, asleep, panic-stricken – or at the very worst, murdered? At that point David thought that his own nerves might be giving way, tapped on the door and pushed it open.

The door to the bedroom was ajar and David could see Gawaine curled up on the bed. He was much more alert than when David had left him; he had got as far as putting on a dressing gown, and he had also acquired a cup of coffee which David eyed covetously.

"Good morning," Gawaine greeted him as he went in. "How was the inquest?"

"Dull. Adjourned for further investigation."

Gawaine shrugged. "As expected." He glanced up at

David, who realised that for some reason he was looking exceptionally smug. "I had a thought."

"Really?" David said. "Guard it well." When Gawaine didn't explain, he added, "Okay, what is it?"

"M, my dear David. M who was Templeman's lunch appointment. I wasn't myself yesterday, or I would have realised it sooner."

"And..?" David prompted, managing not to get annoyed at the way Gawaine was dragging this out. "Don't tell me Templeman was James Bond."

Gawaine blinked up at him, bemused. "Who?"

David refused to be diverted. "Never mind. Who was this M?"

"Templeman has – had – a colleague he worked with closely, on various digs around the Mediterranean, most recently in Turkey," Gawaine replied. "They co-authored a book; actually, it's sitting on my shelves at home even as we speak. Her name, David, is Marcia Scott, and her lair is in Lady Margaret Hall."

"Brilliant!" David had to admit that Gawaine had ample excuse for looking smug. "So she – "

"She is almost certainly our missing M." Gawaine sighed, the smugness dissipating, to leave him looking dissatisfied. "But even if I'm right, it doesn't get us very far, does it?"

"It might," David argued. "Maybe she had a motive for killing him that had nothing to do with the bones."

Gawaine shook his head. "Very untidy, if so. Quite contrary to Occam's Razor. *Pluralitas non est ponenda sine necessitate.*"

"You what?"

"Sorry, my dear David. My classical education coming out again, like a rash. It's a tool in logic: in short, the simplest answer is the best."

David felt like reminding him that real life was often quite messy and not simple at all, but just then he remembered what he had momentarily forgotten in his relief at seeing Gawaine alive and more or less returned to normal – that he had left a highly explosive woman at the bottom of the staircase.

"Listen, Gawaine – " he began.

The outer door opened. A clear voice inquired, "David, what on earth is keeping you?"

Gawaine started, and directed one scorching look at David. A moment later he was all charm as he uncurled himself from the bed and went into the other room to meet Seff. "My dear Persephone! So you're in Oxford. How perfectly delightful! And David brought you to see me. How thoughtful..."

He bestowed a brilliant smile on David, though David knew him well enough to detect the claws beneath the purr, and wondered what he was going to have to say about this afterwards. Then Gawaine turned back to Seff, who was watching them both with undisguised enjoyment.

"Isn't it a good thing I spotted David at the inquest?" she asked. "Now you won't have to creep about looking over your shoulder to see if I'm following you. I'm already here."

"So I see," Gawaine murmured, with an affected shudder. "Although why it should appear to either of you that I intend saying anything to the Press under any circumstances, I do not and never shall understand."

Seff produced one of her most winning looks. "But you will, won't you, Gawaine?"

"They're bound to catch up with you at Templeman's inquest, if not before," David pointed out, uneasily hoping to excuse himself.

"Mmm..." Gawaine paused, his mind idling briefly in neutral, then suddenly shot a glance at David, blue eyes sparking dangerously. "Very well, if that's the way you want it..."

He turned back to Seff, almost over-attentive now, settling her in the most comfortable chair, fussing about whether the light was good enough for her to take notes, offering her coffee.

"I found that the undergraduate who lives here has the makings," he explained. "Instant, of course, but *faute de mieux*... Perhaps you could see to it, David. And remind me to buy him a jar of rather better stuff before we leave."

David did as he was told, while Gawaine finished the preliminaries with Seff, who opened her briefcase and whipped out a notebook and pencil. "Okay, fire ahead," she said.

Seeming quite at ease now, Gawaine launched into the story of what had been happening in St Clement's College. To David, who sat by the window, keeping quiet while he drank his coffee, he seemed a bit too eager, and remembering that dangerous look, David wondered what he was getting up to now.

He found out a little later, as Gawaine began winding up his account by telling Seff about finding Templeman's body. He had said nothing about Porteus having a copy of Templeman's reprint, or about Marcia Scott. David was beginning to think that he could relax, when Gawaine, sounding unusually business-like, said, "And now, Persephone, listen very carefully. Take this down, and you may quote me. I have some evidence about the father of the girl's baby. When I have had a chance to follow this up, I have every hope of being able to identify him."

Seff looked up sharply from her notebook. "Are you sure you want to say that?"

"Positive."

Seff shrugged. "It's your funeral."

"That's just what it will be!" David protested. "When the murderer reads that – "

Gawaine gave him a tight smile. "Exactly."

"Look, I want to talk to you."

"Don't mind me," Seff said with a wave of her hand. "You go right ahead. Gawaine, I told David I would let you vet my piece, so I'll just rough it out now, while you two savage each other."

She moved her chair in front of the desk, extracted a tablet computer out of her briefcase and flipped it open. While she bent her head over it, typing rapidly from her notes, David motioned Gawaine to join him on the other side of the room. "Have you lost your mind?"

Gawaine, arranging himself elegantly on the arm of David's chair, raised his brows but made no other reply. David restrained himself with difficulty from wringing his neck.

"For a start, you *don't* know anything about the baby's father."

"So?" Gawaine murmured. "I doubt Persephone really believes there is any evidence. She thinks I'm just…flying a kite. As I am, of course."

David shook his head. "You have lost your mind."

"No I haven't. I'm just sick and tired of sitting around. I want some action."

"You'll get it. And when you do, you won't like it," David said. "So don't pretend I didn't warn you. Just hope that it doesn't end with you in the morgue."

He fell silent, knowing perfectly well that arguing was useless with Gawaine in this mood. Outside the window, a pigeon pecked its way around the bit of visible roof. Much simpler if you were a pigeon, David thought. Seed, water, fly around a bit, lay the odd egg…and maybe end up as some don's pigeon pie. But at least pigeons, as far as he knew, didn't murder each other.

His ornithological reflections were interrupted by Seff, who had finished her rough draft and brought it over to Gawaine.

David read the screen over his friend's shoulder. There was nothing unexpected about it, until he came to the end, and bit back an exclamation. Seff had left out Gawaine's bait to the murderer.

"I'm sorry, Gawaine," she said, "but that takes the biscuit. If I wrote it, and someone did finish you off, I couldn't live with myself."

David stared at her as if this evidence of a moral code might be written on her face.

Gawaine shrugged apologetically. "Perhaps it was a stupid idea." He did nothing to try to make her change her mind.

David seethed inwardly. All his persuasions had been useless, and now one little nudge from Seff…though he had to be glad, after all, that she had given it.

"Will you have lunch with us later?" Gawaine asked her.

"No, thanks," Seff replied, beginning to pack up her computer. "I'm going to talk to the workmen who found the body, and then see who else is hanging around college. Wish me luck!"

Then she was gone.

"She was quite right," Gawaine said, looking dispirited as he crossed to the table and picked up Seff's abandoned notes. "You were both right. What do you think we should do now?"

David's first reaction was to say, "Nothing," but he knew how that would be received. "We might visit Marcia Scott," he said. "Check up if she really was Templeman's lunch date."

"Very well, my dear David," Gawaine said amenably. "Your word is law."

Ignoring the derisive noise David made, he tossed the notes into the bin and went to get dressed.

Chapter Ten

'Bring candid Eyes unto the perusal of mens works, and let not...Detraction blast well intended labours.'
Christian Morals, II.ii

David felt that lunch time was fast approaching, but Gawaine headed out determinedly and led the way into the University Parks. In the sunlight, with birdsong all around, punctuated by the distant thwack of willow on leather, David felt that murder was very far away. Unfortunately, he knew it would not stay that way for long. Whatever Gawaine might say, David was well aware that they might be about to confront the woman who had killed Richard Templeman.

Emerging at the other side of the Parks, Gawaine turned towards an entrance gateway. At the same moment a woman on a bike rounded a nearby corner and came sailing down the road. Gawaine stiffened suddenly and stepped out in front of her before she could reach the gate.

"Professor Scott?" he said politely.

The woman brought her bike to a halt just in time to avoid mowing Gawaine down. She was about fifty, dumpy and grey-haired, wearing loose cotton trousers and a vaguely oriental-looking jacket. She fixed Gawaine with a stare from pebble-grey eyes. "Do I know you?"

"No. I recognised you from the cover of your book on the Ephesus dig," Gawaine explained. "I found it fascinating."

Marcia Scott looked unimpressed. "Thank you. But I really haven't time to – "

She dismounted from her bike and tried to wheel it around Gawaine and through the gate. He intercepted her again.

"I'm sorry," he began. "But that isn't what I wanted to talk to you about. May we…?" He indicated the gate with a graceful wave of his hand.

"No." Marcia Scott sounded even more abrupt. "I'm extremely busy and – "

"It's about Richard Templeman."

There was definite shock in the woman's expression as she gazed at Gawaine without speaking. David tried to decide whether she looked guilty, or just stunned to be accosted like this by a total stranger.

"You do know..?" Gawaine went on delicately.

"I know Dr Templeman is dead, yes," Professor Scott said. Anger was invading her voice, and her look of shock escalated into a furious glare. "And I have nothing to say about him. Are you from the Press?"

"No," Gawaine replied, shuddering faintly. "I'm sorry, I should have explained. My name is Gawaine St Clair, and I'm here at the request of the Dean of – "

"That has nothing to do with me," Marcia Scott retorted, making another attempt to wheel her bike through the gate.

This time it was David who intercepted her. "Did you have a lunch date with Templeman yesterday?" he asked.

Marcia Scott transferred the glare him. "I have no intention of submitting to an interrogation in the public street," she snapped. "Now, do you mean to let me go about my business, or do I need to call the police?"

David would have given it one more try, but Gawaine caught his arm and drew him aside. "I'm sorry," he said. Without even acknowledging that he had spoken, Marcia Scott and her bike vanished through the gate.

"That went well," David said.

Gawaine let out a long sigh. "Stupid of me," he murmured. "I should have phoned for an appointment instead of stopping her in the street like that. No wonder she sent us off with a flea in our ear."

He cast a final glance through the college gate and turned away, discouragement radiating from him like heatwaves.

"What now?" David asked as they walked up the street. "Food," he added when there was no response from Gawaine.

No more was said about Marcia Scott until they were seated in the Lamb and Flag, investigating the lunch menu. The pub was packed, their low-voiced conversation lost amid the general racket.

"She was rattled when you mentioned Templeman," David pointed out. "Badly rattled."

"I mishandled it," Gawaine said, fixing his dewy glass of Pinot Grigio with a melancholy gaze.

David shook his head. "Maybe, but you can't blame yourself entirely. She was abrupt at first, but as soon as Templeman's name came up, she got furious. I thought she was going to lose it."

Gawaine blinked, considering that. "So?"

"So maybe she did it. She met him for lunch, and – "

"And killed him?" Gawaine's voice was tight. "Why?"

David shrugged. "How should I know? Something academic, maybe. They worked together – closely, if they collaborated on digs and co-authored a book. Aren't these scholarly types always out to cut each other's throats? Maybe Templeman took too much credit."

"And pigs might fly, my dear David." Gawaine gave him a pained look. "I've told you, Templeman wasn't that kind of man. Besides, it's clear from the book that Marcia Scott was the one in charge."

So maybe he attacked her, David thought but didn't say. He knew the sort of response he would get if he did.

"In any case," Gawaine went on, "for that to be true, she would have had to be in St Clement's on Monday when it happened, and no one has mentioned seeing her."

"No one has been asked," David pointed out. "I think we ought to let Inspector Carter know about this."

Gawaine didn't reply, but he clearly didn't favour the idea. Why was it, David asked himself, that his friend always had this instinct to *protect* people? First Porteus, over the reprint, and now Marcia Scott.

Once it was me, he added to himself.

When David and Gawaine returned to college, Heatherington signalled to them from his lair in the lodge.

"Message for you, sir," he said, waving a small white envelope at Gawaine.

Gawaine thanked him and continued into the college garden before halting to tear open the envelope and unfold the single sheet of paper it contained. For a moment he remained staring at it, a faint frown gathering between his brows.

"What is it?" David asked impatiently.

"A note from the Master," Gawaine murmured. "Requesting my presence…'at my earliest convenience.'"

"That means 'right now,'" David translated.

"If not sooner." Gawaine blinked worriedly, then seemed to brace himself. "Well, *carpe diem* and all that."

The Master's rooms were situated at the end of a long passage where the walls were hung with photographs of healthy young men who appeared to have achieved some sporting triumph or killed something both dangerous and decorative. David, whose knowledge of Oxford sport was confined to the Boat Race, let his gaze flick over them with little interest. Gawaine ignored them altogether.

Before Gawaine and David reached the door at the end of the passage it opened and the Master himself appeared, a thin document folder tucked under one arm. When he saw them, he halted.

"St Clair," he said, his tone frosty. "You took your time. You'd better come through."

Gawaine cast a flickering glance at David before following the Master through an outer office guarded by a sleek secretary, and into a large, airy room with French windows opening onto the college garden. On one side was a desk with all the technological accoutrements the wit of man could devise, while the rest of the room was taken up with overstuffed armchairs covered in shiny stripes, and pseudo-antique tables that seemed ready to collapse if you put a cup of coffee on them. To David it looked like the kind of place inhabited by the chairman of some high-powered board, completely lacking in personality.

When they had first met Edwin Galbraith on the Monday evening they had arrived in Oxford, he had been agitated, grasping at straws. He was not agitated now. He offered seats to David and Gawaine with a perfunctory gesture, and snapped out the single word, “Well?”

Gawaine raised his eyebrows in a look of well-bred incomprehension. “Excuse me, Master?”

Galbraith’s pursy little mouth tightened. “What have you to tell me? I’m bound to say, St Clair, I expected you to report to me before now.”

“When I have something to report, I shall do so,” Gawaine responded. “These things take time.”

“It’s time the College may not have,” the Master said, beginning to pace fretfully. “At all costs we should avoid a scandal.”

Good luck with that, David thought.

“I really don’t believe – ” Gawaine began.

“What will our funding bodies think?” Galbraith interrupted, swinging around at the far end of the room and glaring at Gawaine. “St Clement’s is a centre of academic excellence. Digging up bodies is not part of our remit.”

David stifled a snigger at that, though he was sure the Master had not intended to be funny.

“I’m sure it’s not part of anyone’s remit,” Gawaine replied. “It is, however, a fact that the body was found – ”

“In our garden, yes.” Galbraith resumed pacing. “But it’s quite inconceivable that anyone connected with St Clement’s was responsible for putting it there. This College has always prided itself on attracting men of the highest integrity."

And one murderer, David thought. "Are we falling back on that old stand-by, the passing tramp?" he asked.

Galbraith's gaze flicked toward him and away again as if dismissing his remark, and indeed David himself, as negligible. "You should make that the thrust of your inquiry," he told Gawaine.

"The passing tramp? Or the men of highest integrity?" Gawaine spoke in tones of silken courtesy, the sign to David that he had passed from confusion to incandescent anger, which would never, ever be permitted to surface. "I'm sure, Master, you wouldn't want to prejudice the investigation in any way."

Galbraith let out an irritated snort. "You should look at what's staring you in the face," he snapped. "It's quite impossible that any of us should be responsible for this body, and the sooner you can make the police see that, the better. Why do you think you're here?"

Gawaine exchanged a brief glance with David. "I'm sorry, Master," he said, "but I rather thought that I was here to discover the truth."

"Truth!" The Master put a world of contempt into one word. "Can't you see that what happened thirty years ago is far less important than what will happen here and now if we don't clear up this affair quickly?"

Gawaine blinked. "What is truth, said jesting Pilate, and would not stay for an answer," he quoted. Rising to his feet, he added, "I think we're done here, Master."

"We're done when I say we are," Galbraith retorted. "This is my College, St Clair, and don't you forget it. I have to say that I didn't approve at all of Stephen Verner calling you in without consulting me first. Most inappropriate."

"You didn't seem to think that on Monday night," David pointed out, rising to stand beside Gawaine.

The Master shrugged that off, a petulant gesture. He was an essentially weak man, David thought, wielding power like a club with a nail in it.

"Very well," he said. "We will end this meeting here. But you will report to me, St Clair, and you will do everything in your power to minimise the impact of this disgraceful affair on the College. Do you understand?"

"Quite clearly, Master."

"Then you may go."

Dismissed, with the outer door of Galbraith's suite between them and the Master, Gawaine said nothing, but let out a long breath.

"No pressure, then," David remarked.

For a moment Gawaine did not reply, only beginning to walk slowly down the passage toward the door that led out into the garden.

"He really doesn't want you here," David continued, pacing along beside him under the gaze of the athletic young men in the photographs. "Cross him, and you'll find yourself out on your ear." And that could be a good thing, he thought. Except that now David knew Gawaine wouldn't give up, and if the Master did throw him out of college he would hole up somewhere until he had found the answer.

Gawaine dismissed the Master with an airy wave of one hand. "He can rant all he likes, my dear David, but the facts of this case will surface sooner or later, and he won't like it."

"Come to that, he won't like it tomorrow when Seff's paper comes out," David said.

Gawaine gave a faint, cat-like smile. "Indeed. I can't wait." Reaching the garden door, he halted and added, "I need to wander off for a while and have a think. Don't you have financial markets to prop up, or something of that sort?"

"I have contracts to work on, yes," David responded. "But if you're going off alone, make sure you wander somewhere safe. Out of college, for a start."

Gawaine nodded. "Don't worry. I shall go and watch the cricket. Always so soothing, don't you think? Meet me in the lodge at seven, and we'll go for dinner."

Chapter Eleven

'I could be content that we might procreate like trees, without conjunction, or that there were any way to perpetuate the World without this trivial and vulgar way of union.'

Religio Medici

If Gawaine's communing with the cricket match in the Parks had produced any results, he did not share them with David. Dinner was punctuated by airy conversation on subjects ranging from the Van Gogh exhibition at the Tate to the care and nurturing of cats, and the St Clement's body was not mentioned at all. David wondered what their next move should be. He couldn't see any way ahead.

Gawaine was silent as they returned to their rooms in college and paused outside his door. "Good night, David."

"What happens tomorrow?" David asked.

"I'm not sure..."

Gawaine's voice died away. One hand fastened around David's wrist. David's question also died as he saw what Gawaine was looking at. A line of light was visible under the door. They exchanged a glance; then, after a second's nervous hesitation, Gawaine straightened up and released David, turned the knob and went in.

There was a woman in the room. Fictional detectives,

David reflected, often returned to their rooms or flats or country houses and discovered a glamorous female supine on their bed. He had always thought of it as one of the perks of the job.

This particular woman, however, was neither glamorous nor supine. She was Marcia Scott: not a woman, as such, but another scholar. There were, in David's view, far too many of them about. He exchanged an edgy glance with Gawaine; had she come to berate him again in his own room?

But Marcia Scott was smiling as she rose from the armchair by the window. She said in a voice that, now she wasn't out for blood, was deep and remarkably attractive, "I'm afraid I've given you a shock."

"Slightly," Gawaine admitted. He had started breathing again. "What can I – "

"Your door wasn't locked," she interrupted, showing some nervousness herself. "So I thought I'd wait. I wanted to talk to you. To begin with, I owe you an apology."

"Certainly not," Gawaine responded. "It was entirely my fault. I should have telephoned you first."

"If you had, I should have refused to see you. But I've spoken to Stephen Verner since then, and I've had some time to think..." She paused and then went on, "What did you want to ask me about Richard Templeman?"

Gawaine took a deep breath. He was disconcerted, David could see, by this complete about-face. "Dr Templeman had a lunch appointment last Monday with someone named M," he said at last. "Was that you?"

Professor Scott nodded. "I'd invited him to Lady Margaret Hall because we were due to leave in a week's time to take part in the next phase of the Ephesus dig, and we needed to discuss the final arrangements." Her voice shook suddenly. "He never came."

At least, that's your story, David thought, though he doubted she would have told such a blatant lie if she had come to meet Templeman at St Clement's. Someone would be bound to have seen her there.

Gawaine nodded slowly. "Thank you. That does help."

With the question asked and answered, David expected Professor Scott to take her leave. Instead, she stayed where she was, her gaze unfocused, as if she was mulling something over in her mind.

"There's something else..." she said after a few moments. "Something I think you ought to know."

"Yes?" Gawaine said encouragingly.

"Richard and I were very good friends." Marcia Scott sat down again, and Gawaine took the chair beside her, waiting for her to go on. "I may as well tell you," she said at last, "that he had been asking me to marry him for the last thirty years."

Thirty years, David thought. *The same length of time that the woman has been buried in the garden. Coincidence?*

"You turned him down?" he asked, worming his way into the conversation rather against his better judgement.

Marcia Scott seemed to realise for the first time that there was a third person in the room, and Gawaine hastily introduced him, though the cursory glance and conventional greeting she gave David showed that she was not really interested. It was to Gawaine that she replied.

"We worked together. I always considered my work

more important than marriage. I refused his proposals because I refused to accept the demands on my time that marriage and children would have made."

There were not many people, David thought, who would start to give you all the details of their marriage or lack of marriage so soon after meeting you. Marcia Scott must be unique. Or perhaps it was a question of who you gave it to. Gawaine seemed to invite these confidences. It was he who was unique – but then, David had known that all along.

"I'm telling you this," Professor Scott explained, "because I want you to understand that Richard and I were close, and he trusted me. He gave me something, a long time ago, and now..." She hesitated again. "Now I don't know what to do with it."

She opened her bag and took out an envelope. An ordinary brown manila envelope.

"Years ago, Richard gave me this. He said he thought it might be important, and I could see it worried him. He didn't tell me what it is, but he said it was something he didn't want to keep in his rooms here in college, and would I keep it for him. So I did."

"And if he died in mysterious circumstances – " David began eagerly.

Professor Scott shook her head impatiently. "Nothing of the kind. He simply asked me to keep it for him. But now he is dead – in mysterious circumstances, if you wish to use that phrase – I don't know what to do with it." She turned back to Gawaine. "Going to the police seems rather extreme. Stephen Verner explained to me how you were here, keeping an eye on things for the College, so I thought I would give it to you."

She held out the envelope. Gawaine looked at it, fascinated, but made no move to take it.

"You don't know what it is?" he asked.

"No. Nor do I want to," she added in a more decisive tone. Whatever it is, it has nothing to do with me. I restrict my curiosity to my work." She offered the envelope again. "Are you going to take it?"

This time Gawaine accepted it. "With the understanding," he said, "that I reserve the right to pass it on to the police if it should seem necessary."

"Of course." Though Professor Scott seemed to have nothing more to say, she did not move from the armchair.

Tentatively Gawaine said, "It must have been a great shock to you, to hear that Dr Templeman was dead. I'm sorry."

"A shock?" Marcia Scott's manner had grown more abrupt. "Yes, it was a shock. And at my time of life one prefers not to have to question decisions made almost thirty years ago. I ask myself, if I had married Richard, would it have been different?"

Gawaine said nothing to that. There was not very much to say. David could see that if Templeman had been married, he would have been safely in the bosom of his family, not being shoved down a flight of stairs in an Oxford College.

"I made the choice," Professor Scott continued, "but was it the right one? There would have been children."

"Your work is very valuable," Gawaine offered delicately. "Your books..."

"Stephen Verner tells me you're a classicist, Mr St Clair. You remember Cornelia Graccha? She was poor, but she could say, 'My children are my jewels.' How tragic if it had been the other way round. 'My jewels are my children.' If I had Richard's children, this would be easier now." She got to her feet. "Good night, Mr St Clair."

Gawaine followed her to the door, closed it behind her, and remained momentarily leaning against it.

"Listen!" David exclaimed, dying to get his theory out as soon as their visitor had gone. "I knew there was something fishy about her! Suppose the girl – the one in the garden – was Templeman's girl. And Marcia Scott was jealous because although she'd turned him down, she didn't want him to have anyone else. So she killed her, and he helped her to bury the body because he loved her and he didn't want her copped! It all fits!"

Gawaine turned back from the door. He looked drained, exhausted. David suddenly regretted being quite so enthusiastic.

"Oh, yes, my dear David, it all fits," Gawaine said tiredly. "Psychologically it's quite convincing. Congratulations."

"But?"

Gawaine blinked. "But?"

"There was a but in your voice."

Gawaine gave the ghost of the elegant shrug he had practised in the Delphinium Walk. "It explains the girl's murder quite nicely, but how do you explain Templeman's?"

"She wasted him as well…because…" This bit wasn't quite so easy. "Because the body had turned up and he was going to spill the beans."

"What a masterly grasp of cliché you have, my dear David. It must be quite invaluable to you in your line of work. All you need to do now is explain why he should so picturesquely spill the beans after thirty years when the trail was cold, and how she managed to do it, because as I said before, no one has mentioned seeing her in college on Monday. You might poison someone in your absence, but to push someone downstairs you have to be on the spot."

While David thought about that, Gawaine drifted back across the room and picked up the envelope which he had abandoned on the arm of his chair. Staring at it with a bewildered expression, he sank wearily into the seat again.

"Her anger this morning wasn't guilt, but grief. Losing him was the worst thing that could happen to her, the thing you always tell yourself will never happen. Also," he continued more practically, "she would hardly bring me this if she had killed him."

"You don't know what it is," David objected. "You only have her word that Templeman gave it to her."

Gawaine nodded. "True."

He began teasing delicately at the flap of the envelope until he got it open and then very carefully slid out what it contained, a single sheet of writing paper.

"A letter?" David asked.

"Yes – no. Part of a letter."

Gawaine bent his head over the sheet, which he held by the very edges. David had no need to ask why, though he wondered if fingerprints would survive for that length of time. Impatiently he waited while Gawaine read it.

"What does it say?"

There was no reply for a few seconds. Then: "It's the end of a letter, David. It starts in the middle of a sentence. '…thought of a good name yet? If we have a boy, I like

John for a second name, but he would need something more distinguished to start with. Would you like him to be a soldier like his Dad? I'm feeling well, and Something John is kicking harder every day. I only wish I could see more of you, but we've got the vacation to look forward to. With all my love, Sue.'" Gawaine looked up at David with a blank expression. "Well, at least we can put a name to her."

David reached out for the sheet of paper and Gawaine gave it to him; he remembered to be careful of fingerprints. As he read the letter over again, he said slowly, "She's pregnant, so she's presumably the girl in the garden. It sounds as if she's writing to the father, but... What's the matter?"

Gawaine had suddenly turned away. When he spoke, his voice was shaking. "It's such a *happy* letter, David. She wants her baby. She's in love with the father. And then she comes here and he kills her."

David looked down at him sombrely. He knew that the last chance – if there had ever been a chance – of persuading Gawaine to give up had just vanished. If David was right, his friend was about to embark on a personal crusade on behalf of a dead girl called Sue. And for all Gawaine's airs and graces, David would not have fancied being in the murderer's shoes just then.

"But look," he began, hoping that a problem would help Gawaine pull himself together, "there's something here that doesn't add up."

Gawaine looked up, in control again. "Oh, you noticed that, my dear David? That socking great anomaly in the middle of our nice, tidy theories? 'Would you like him to be a soldier like his Dad?' All very well, but the only one of our suspects you could describe as being a soldier is Colonel Morrison. And we had managed to eliminate him."

Chapter Twelve

''Tis an easie and necessary belief, to credit what our eye and sense hath examined.'

Religio Medici

After breakfast the following morning, Gawaine tried to get in touch with Inspector Carter. But his phone call to the police station revealed that the Inspector was out, and so he and David decided to tackle the Bursar's wife at her home in North Oxford.

Gawaine, however, would talk about anything but that. "Very high-powered, the science here," he remarked as they strolled north along the edge of the Oxford Science Area. "Or so I'm led to believe. Naturally, I don't speak from personal experience. I shouldn't even recognise the sound of an atom splitting."

David murmured something. When Gawaine was in this vein of trivial chatter, he tended to relegate it to pleasant background noise.

"Of course," Gawaine continued, "one feels obliged to accept that scientists may be quite civilised. Many of them, for example, seem to have been very fond of cats – always a sign of civilisation, don't you agree? Sir Isaac Newton, Schrödinger… I have often felt – "

"Do you think Morrison killed the girl?"

Gawaine stopped, thought, and then walked on again. He did not reply for a moment, but his reflections on modern science were lost for ever.

"I really don't know," he replied after a while. "There is the letter… And yet, at the time, he was an undergraduate, and you would hardly think that getting a girl pregnant would drive him to murder."

"Unless she was pressing for marriage, and he thought it would ruin his career."

Gawaine looked sceptical. "In the army? Besides, that letter sounds as if Sue thinks the father wants the baby just as much as she does. Mind you," he added, "if it was Morrison, and if the police are right about her age, then she was older than he was, though not by much. I wonder if that might have a bearing?"

"Student involved with an older woman?" David said. "Sounds normal. Learning about life."

Gawaine winced. "Life, my dear David," he said, "is usually more complicated. What do you think goes on in our institutions of learning? Besides, the type of woman you have in mind, if indeed she exists, presumably has the expertise not to get pregnant unless she wants to."

He fell silent. They walked on and reached the residential areas of North Oxford, where all the houses, as Gawaine remarked, look like rectories. It was here that the Bursar lived.

"What tale are you going to tell?" David asked.

"Tale?" Gawaine frowned, considering. David suspected that the thought of what he was going to say to Mrs Bursar had not previously crossed his mind. "Ask to read the gas meter?"

David gave that proposal the best possible response by totally ignoring it.

"We might try the truth?" Gawaine suggested delicately.

The conversation came to an abrupt end as they reached the Morrisons' house. Gawaine led the way up the path and rang the bell. While they waited, David took stock; it was an old house, Victorian, but freshly painted and in good repair. At the sound of the doorbell a dog started barking inside, and when the door opened the woman standing there was stooping with her hand in the collar of a cocker spaniel.

"Shut up, you horrible beast," she said; David assumed she was addressing the dog. "Hello," she added. "What can I do for you?"

Gawaine introduced the two of them.

"Oh, yes," the woman said, before he had the chance to tell any tale, true or not. "Michael told me about you. Come in. Do you mind the kitchen?"

They followed her into the passage into a large, sunlit room, painted yellow, with a tiled floor. Their hostess let the dog into the back garden with a parting pat; it lolloped across the lawn to a climbing frame where two track-suited children were playing.

"Sorry," she said. "Coffee?"

As she put on the percolator, David had his first chance of a proper look at her. She was small, dark, and very slight and quick-moving. He guessed she was in her late thirties. He also guessed she was highly intelligent – perhaps too intelligent for comfort.

Her first words caused him to delete the 'perhaps'.

"You've come to ask me where Michael was on Monday morning?"

Gawaine, as he accepted the seat she offered him at the scrubbed pine kitchen table, looked slightly taken aback.

Mrs Morrison grinned faintly. "It's all right," she said. "The police have already been here. And I know you're doing what you can for the College. Ask me what you like."

Gawaine looked relieved as he took her at her word. David could see that he was relaxing, at ease in his surroundings. "That was the morning Colonel Morrison had his stomach upset?"

Mrs Morrison had turned away, and was setting out mugs on the work surface next to the kettle. "That's right," she replied. "I don't know what caused it, but I expect it was something he ate in college, because the kids and I were all right. He was up half Sunday night, and on Monday morning I just told him to stay in bed. I rang the college, as you know."

"What time was that?"

"When I rang? Just after nine o'clock."

"Did the doctor say what the matter was?" Gawaine asked.

"Michael wouldn't have the doctor. He never will – I suppose it's all this army stuff, stiff upper lip and what have you. I would have called him, but by teatime Michael was looking better, and of course he was back in college the day after."

"Did you think he was fit to go to work?"

David did not entirely see the point of that question; Mrs Morrison looked rather puzzled, but she answered readily enough.

"He looked a bit green, but yes, I suppose he was fit enough."

"And were you with him all of Monday morning?" Gawaine added tentatively.

That was the question, David thought, at which any loving wife ought to have taken offence. The implication was that if she had not had her eye on her husband all day, he might have sneaked off into college and murdered Templeman.

Mrs Morrison, however, took it in her stride. "I was in the house all morning," she answered, turning to pour the coffee. "Usually I wouldn't be, but I teach at the Dragon School, and our term ended last week."

Gawaine nodded, accepting his coffee and gently dissuading her from adulterating it with milk. "So the Colonel couldn't have gone into college without your knowing?"

"I told the police, Mr St Clair, Michael was nowhere near college on Monday morning. And another thing – " She put a biscuit barrel on the table and took her own coffee, sitting at the table opposite Gawaine and David. "I didn't marry Michael until well after that girl was buried in the garden, but I've known him all my life. I don't think he could possibly have had anything to do with it."

That was no more than the reference any wife should have given her husband, David thought. His expression must have given him away, for Mrs Morrison glanced at him sharply, and said, "I'm not trying to tell you he's perfect. But if he did do wrong, it wouldn't be that. Do you understand?"

"Yes, of course," Gawaine responded, and added with apparent irrelevance, "Has Colonel Morrison been a professional soldier all his life?"

Mrs Morrison looked slightly startled, and her tone as she replied showed that this was another question she didn't see the point of. "Yes, until a couple of years ago. He comes from an old army family."

"He did a degree at St Clement's, I believe?"

"Yes, Maths. Though he was involved with the army even then. OTC and so on." She drank coffee, hesitated, and then added, "To be honest, I don't think his family left him with much choice. It's only recently that I've talked him round to seeing that there might be more in life than waving the flag."

Here was someone else, David thought, letting Gawaine in on her personal life after a very short acquaintance. He was responding, sympathising with the problems and limitations of reconciling family life with a military career, and effectively bringing the interrogation to an end.

They stayed for a while longer, finishing the coffee and chatting of this and that – Mrs Morrison's school, the state of the universities, and the cultivation of clematis – as if Gawaine had nothing more serious on his mind. They parted friends: Mrs Morrison made, and Gawaine accepted, an invitation to dinner on the Saturday evening.

"You don't think he did it," David said, as they made their way back to the centre of Oxford in search of yet another pub lunch.

"What makes you think that?"

"You wouldn't dream of going to dinner with a murderer."

Gawaine gave him a rather intense look, as if the remark was unexpected. "No," he conceded. "And yet…"

"Yet what?"

"I felt it was – not…not quite right. She was too pleasant, and she said just a bit too much. 'The lady doth protest too much, methinks.'"

"Eh?"

Gawaine sighed. "Hamlet, my dear David. The Player Queen. Another lady who had too much to say for herself. You would be more prickly, wouldn't you, if someone suggested your nearest and dearest went around tipping people down staircases?"

"Maybe."

"And that stomach upset," Gawaine went on, sounding more focused with every moment that passed. "Morrison looked perfectly all right when we saw him on Tuesday. Certainly not green. I was rather hoping to find that his wife and the children had been laid low as well. Not out of any animosity," he added, forestalling David's question, "but no one in college had it, either."

"How do you know?"

"Don't you remember, the Dean was talking about it on High Table? And suggesting that they had all been eating fricasséed moggie?" He shuddered delicately. "It's an odd stomach upset that doesn't affect anyone else eating at the same table. Possible, but…"

His voice trailed off. After a moment, he sighed once more. He was not looking particularly happy, and David had a good idea why. Scratch Gawaine, and you found a sentimentalist, and he was clearly under the spell of dog, children and sunlit garden, and, purely as an observer, the conversation of an attractive woman. He would not want to disturb the pretty picture, or take kindly to being reminded that it was not all that pretty if the head of the household was a double murderer. Gawaine had very little use for reality.

"He was a soldier from his cradle," he said after a while.

"Therefore making sense of Sue's letter," David contributed.

Gawaine gave him a sombre look, as if the contribution was unwelcome, though he could hardly have failed to draw the same conclusion for himself. "'A soldier like his Dad,'" he mused. "And Colonel Morrison is the only suspect who fits. I suppose it's just about possible that Father Gerard is old enough to have done National Service, but if so he would have finished with it long before Sue wrote her letter. We can forget about that." He frowned thoughtfully. "*Militat omnis amans, et habet sua castra Cupido…*" he murmured.

"Eh?"

"Sorry, my dear David. I tend to forget you haven't had the advantage of a thorough grounding in dead languages," he added with a gleam of amusement. "It's Ovid. 'Every lover is a soldier, and Cupid has his own camp.' But that doesn't get us very far, does it?"

David had no response to make. The quotation didn't seem to have any relevance at all to Sue's letter or their search for a soldier.

"There's one thing," Gawaine remarked rather more brightly.

"What's that?"

They were passing the Science Area again. David listened carefully for the sound of splitting atoms.

"Mrs Morrison's phone call, my dear David," Gawaine went on. You'll recall that she rang first thing in the morning – therefore, before the bones were discovered, and before Templeman was killed. In other words, she gave him an alibi before she knew he would need one. So she must be telling the truth."

"Unless he knew the bones would come to light once the workmen started to dig," David said discouragingly.

Gawaine looked slightly less bright. "There is that. But no – really!" The note of protest in his voice grew more definite. "You're saying that Morrison came into college and murdered Templeman just on the off-chance?"

David shrugged. Personally he wouldn't have been surprised. If Morrison had known the bones would turn up, if he had known the conclusions Templeman would draw... Weren't soldiers supposed to act swiftly, with initiative?

"They didn't call the doctor," he pointed out.

"True. No one to confirm what they say. But there's no one to disprove it, either. And you can't get round the fact that Mrs Morrison rang before the bones were dug up."

That was obviously the way he wanted it, and David did not say any more.

Chapter Thirteen

'Light, that makes things seen, makes some things invisible.'

The Garden of Cyrus, Ch 4

David watched impatiently as Inspector Carter stared at Sue's letter, laid flat on his desk. After a while the Inspector lifted his head and stared at Gawaine. Gawaine avoided that long, unsettling look, and stared at the plant on Carter's desk, which appeared to be flourishing.

"Tell me again how you came by this," Carter said.

Gawaine repeated the account he had already given of Marcia Scott's visit, clearly making a massive effort to sound crisp and efficient, a world away from his usual vagueness.

Carter listened without interruption. "And she said nothing to you of where Templeman found this?" he asked when Gawaine had finished.

Gawaine shook his head. "She implied that he told her nothing about it."

"I'll have to see her." Carter studied the letter again. "A soldier like his Dad..." he mused. "That would seem to point to your Bursar...whatsisname, Morrison."

"He wasn't a soldier then," Gawaine told him; David realised he was choosing to omit all they had discovered about Morrison's early connections with the army. "He was an undergraduate. Surely he wouldn't have committed a murder?"

Carter made an unidentifiable noise, suggesting that he was less than impressed with that line of argument. "We talked to him and his wife," he said. "He seems to have an alibi, but it only rests on her word. He might be worth a closer look. We'll check whether anyone saw him in college when he was supposed to be at home sick."

Gawaine exchanged a glance with David. He was looking faintly distressed, but he said nothing more, not even informing the Inspector that he and David had also been to visit Mrs Morrison. The silence lengthened as Carter gave his attention to the letter again.

"Knowing Templeman, Inspector…" Gawaine began hesitantly.

"Yes."

"We're assuming, are we not, that he knew something about this girl, and he was killed because he confronted her murderer with it?"

"Seems reasonable," the Inspector replied.

"Now, Templeman was a very honest and straightforward man. And he expected the same honesty in others. I shouldn't call him naïf, Inspector, but he would trust you until he saw good reason not to. Do you understand?"

Carter nodded with a faint grin. "I wish I could afford to do the same."

"So," Gawaine continued, "if the murderer explained to Templeman where the girl had gone, Templeman would believe him if there was no other evidence. I think this letter was other evidence."

"But the letter doesn't tell us anything," David protested, breaking in for the first time. "Unless the 'soldier' is Morrison, and even then the letter doesn't prove it."

"Remember, my dear David, Templeman knew more than we do," Gawaine pointed out. "Something in this letter meant something to him. Not proof, of course, or it would all have come out long ago. But something – something made him uneasy. Something that wasn't quite right. So he kept the letter, but because he wanted to be absolutely sure that no one in college would ever see it, he gave it to Professor Scott to keep for him. We can assume, knowing now that murder was done, that this letter constitutes evidence."

"And in that case," Carter said, "we have to ask whether Templeman told his murderer that he had it."

Gawaine started, his eyes widening in alarm. "If he did – " He broke off, relaxing again. "No. Templeman died on Monday morning. If his murderer knew about the letter, he would have made an approach to Professor Scott before now."

The Inspector's grin was more pronounced, almost savage. "'Made an approach.' God, I like that. What it must be, to be a scholar. I'd better go and see her right away." He scribbled a note on his scratch pad. "And I'll get the letter down to the lab. It may be able to tell us a lot. Thank you, Mr St Clair. I don't suppose she would ever have brought it directly to us." Looking up at Gawaine, he continued, "Marcia Scott. Would she by any chance be our mysterious M?"

Reluctantly, Gawaine nodded. "She says that Templeman was supposed to have lunch with her in Lady Margaret Hall, but he never turned up."

"Because of being dead. I see." Inspector Carter made another note. "I'll make sure that gets checked. If she went to St Clement's, someone must have seen her. And the same applies to Colonel Morrison."

They were on their feet and making their farewells when he added, "Tell me, Mr St Clair, what brings you into this sort of thing in the first place?"

Gawaine stiffened. David waited for an answer that was not an answer. He was not disappointed.

"Pure nosiness, Inspector," Gawaine said airily, and led the way out.

Walking back to college, Gawaine was obviously in deep thought, his gaze inward and faintly troubled. David refrained from disturbing him, while thinking wistfully of all the places where one could spend a few free days in summer, more pleasantly than in an Oxford College beset with bodies: Brighton, Biarritz, Runcorn and Widnes...

"Morrison is the only person that letter can point to," David remarked at last.

Gawaine turned to him, blinking as if he had been rudely snatched back from somewhere a very long way away. The remark had been clearly unwelcome.

"Not necessarily," Gawaine replied at last. "I hope the Inspector will check if any of our other suspects have service records. Though I've got a feeling it won't be as easy as that... And it's just occurred to me. We might do something with John."

"Who's John?"

Gawaine gave him a look of severe disapproval. "John, my dear David. John in the letter. John that was to be the baby's second name. It struck me that one very often calls a little boy after his grandfather."

"So if any of our five had a father called John…"

"…it might be interesting. Quite. Of course," Gawaine added discouragingly, "John could have been *her* father."

They arrived at the porter's lodge at the same time as Father Gerard, cassocked and pushing a bicycle. He greeted them so benignly that David felt sure he had an ulterior motive. When he had handed over his conveyance – an ancient iron contraption of the sit-up-and-beg variety – to the porter, he said to Gawaine, "It's time we had a talk, my dear fellow. Why don't you come – both of you, of course – to my rooms for a cup of tea? It is perhaps a little early, but on a warm day like this… I remember, Gawaine, you had a particular fondness for Earl Grey."

Gawaine accepted with every outward sign of pleasure, and David, who had been included but not consulted, tagged on behind. If nothing else, it would be a good opportunity to find out what alibi, if any, Father Gerard had to offer.

"I was talking earlier to a young friend of yours," Father Gerard said as he led them through the college grounds to his rooms. "A young lady. Most attractive. A Miss Brown, I believe she said." Unseen, David gaped. "A newspaper reporter, I understand," Father Gerard rambled on gently. "A most enterprising career for a young lady. We had a delightful chat, all about Common Worship and the latest translations of the Bible. She had some most interesting ideas."

David found it impossible to imagine Seff as a good daughter of the Church, though it occurred to him that if Father Gerard still had an eye for a pretty girl, it might have led him thirty years ago – celibate priest or not – into the sort of indiscretion that could have ended in murder. He wondered whether Gawaine, who was responding in kind to Father Gerard's chit-chat, was taking him at all seriously as a suspect.

The chaplain's sitting room was what David was coming to expect: book-lined, comfortable, slightly shabby, and refreshingly cool after the walk through the hot streets from the police station. The only evidence of Father Gerard's calling was an icon of the Virgin and Child upon one wall.

Gawaine and David seated themselves while Father Gerard fussed around happily making tea.

"A terrible business," he began when preparations were well under way, "about poor Templeman. His sister is in Oxford. I have just been to visit her at her hotel."

Gawaine murmured politely, a shadow of sadness crossing his face at the thought of Templeman's bereaved sister.

"And I understand that you actually found his body," the chaplain went on. "That must have been a very great shock to you."

"Yes. Perfectly frightful." Gawaine's light tone, at odds with his words, told David that he was trying to hide how distressed he had been.

Father Gerard's sympathetic expression suggested that the attempt had failed. "Of course," he said. With meticulous care he poured hot water onto tea leaves. "Most upsetting, especially on your first visit to College for so long. I trust that in spite of everything it won't be your last?"

Gawaine murmured something, avoiding the direct question. David was once again aware of an undercurrent he did not understand, but he was diverted from it by being presented with a delicate cup filled with a fluid that he would never have designated as tea.

"Manna from heaven!" the chaplain pronounced with great satisfaction. "And a Bath Oliver biscuit? These are troubled times, but I find great comfort in a Bath Oliver biscuit."

David declined, sipped, and sipped again. Hmm. Interesting. If he wasn't careful, he might actually get to like the stuff.

Meanwhile, Father Gerard had seated himself with his own tea, and suddenly seemed to drop the pose of saintly idiot with which he had been amusing himself up to now.

"Well, my dear fellow," he said to Gawaine, "I assume you want to know what I was doing last Monday morning?"

Gawaine looked taken aback, as he had at Mrs Morrison's direct approach.

Father Gerard, appearing shrewder now, but not without a twinkle, went on, "That is why you're here, is it not?"

"Unfortunately, yes, Father," Gawaine admitted.

Father Gerard nodded. "Unfortunately. How much more pleasant to discuss the iniquities of modern liturgy. However, since we must..." He set aside his tea-cup to remove his glasses and give them a thorough polishing with a snowy handkerchief. "I got up at seven, meditated here for a while, and then said early Mass in Chapel at eight o'clock. Poor Templeman was there, and afterwards he and I went into breakfast together. That was the last time I saw him."

He paused, sighing with apparently sincere regret, and continued, "I left the refectory at…oh, between nine and nine thirty, and collected my post from the lodge. Heatherington was on duty at the time, as I recall. I returned here, dealt with one letter that needed an urgent reply, checked my email, and then went down to Chapel."

"And then?" David asked.

Father Gerard fitted his glasses upon his nose and peered mildly at David over the top. "I must have stayed there about an hour," he continued. "At any rate, it was just after eleven when I left, and I found the College in an uproar because by that time the bones of that unfortunate girl had been discovered in the garden. I went to speak to the Dean, to see if I could be of any assistance, and I don't think I was out of sight of some member of the College until lunch – which, as always, was at one. I trust you will find that helpful?"

"Admirably clear, Father," Gawaine replied.

David latched onto what he thought of as the one gaping hole in the account he had just heard. "Tell me… er…Father," he asked, "what were you doing in the chapel for an hour?"

Father Gerard gave him a faintly surprised look, as if he could not see why anyone should need to ask that question. "Praying, my dear chap."

"And was anyone else there at that time?" Gawaine asked, coming to the rescue.

The chaplain shook his head. "No. It was a weekday, of course, but all the same, I'm afraid the College is becoming sadly secular."

David was not sure he believed any of that. It was obvious that Father Gerard could easily have found an opportunity to murder Templeman. Perhaps Templeman had come to the chapel deliberately to tax the chaplain with his sins. And then…but the chapel was on the ground floor. No stairs to throw anyone down. Unless there was a crypt… But then why would Templeman have ended up in the trunk room? It would have been beyond Father Gerard's strength to have carried him there. And Inspector Carter had said that Templeman was killed on his own stair.

Meanwhile, Gawaine had launched into another line of questioning. "You were here, Father, at the time the girl would have been buried in the garden?"

Father Gerard considered. "Thirty years, I believe? Yes, I was here. Do you know, I shall have been chaplain of St Clement's for thirty-two years on the feast day of St Simon and St Jude."

Whenever that might be, David thought.

"But you know nothing about her?" Gawaine asked.

"Nothing at all. Though I have remembered her in my prayers. She must have been extremely unhappy."

David saw a slight frown crease Gawaine's brows, only momentarily, but he knew his friend must be thinking of the happiness of that letter.

"And Templeman said nothing to you about her – then or later?"

For a moment Father Gerard looked shocked. "But Richard Templeman would never – oh, I see what you mean. He knew something about her, and that's why the poor fellow was killed. No, he – yes, now I come to think about it, there was something."

Gawaine leant forward, all affectations forgotten. "Yes?"

Father Gerard drained his teacup. "He came to me – yes, it must have been about that time. Of course, he was younger than I, just appointed to his Fellowship. He told me that he suspected that something discreditable was going on in College, but he had no proof. What should he do, he asked me."

"And you told him?"

"I told him to do nothing. Without proof, anything he might say would be only slander." Father Gerard smiled reminiscently. "I remember I sent him away to read the Epistle of James. And I told him to come to me again if he discovered anything definite. But he never mentioned the matter after that."

"And he gave you no indication of what he was talking about?" Gawaine asked.

"None whatsoever. It would, of course, have been very wrong of him to do so."

Gawaine nodded. His brief flash of animation died away, leaving him looking discouraged.

"Your investigations are not bearing fruit?" Father Gerard asked.

"No. I'm acquiring a lot of information – and I'm very grateful, Father, for what you've told me – but none of it seems to be leading me anywhere. Or rather, some of it seems to be leading me in quite the wrong direction. Perhaps you could invoke a suitable saint."

Father Gerard seemed to accept this as a spiritual witticism. "Yes, indeed. St Anthony might possibly be appropriate. I think not St Jude – or at least, not yet. The patron saint of lost causes," he added in explanation to David. "Although a classicist like yourself, Gawaine," he continued, "might prefer to consider a quiet word with Juno – who you may remember had a particular sympathy with pregnant women. More tea?"

Chapter Fourteen

'These are niceties that become not those that peruse so serious a Mystery.'
Religio Medici

When they had taken leave of Father Gerard, David could not resist asking, "Do you believe that he was praying for an hour in the chapel?"

"I see no reason not to," Gawaine replied abstractedly. "It goes, as one might say, with the job. Of course, my dear David, I realise it doesn't constitute an alibi. I rather doubt that the Almighty will be available to corroborate it."

They stepped through an archway into another part of the college gardens, a wide stretch of perfectly rolled turf ending in a row of lime trees. A couple of dons were pottering over something at the other side of the lawn.

Gawaine paused. "There was something he said that interested me."

"Yes?"

"When he was telling us about Templeman coming to ask for advice – you remember? Templeman said that he had discovered something discreditable going on in College. Now, assuming that Father Gerard was quoting his exact words, do you really think he would describe the suspected murder of someone's pregnant mistress as 'something discreditable'?"

David shrugged. "I don't do don-speak."

"It sounds more like cheating at cards," Gawaine went on. "Or, given the academic environment, fiddling an exam. And it sounds more like an ongoing situation than a single act. Whatever, not murder, surely?"

"Then perhaps Templeman was referring to something else altogether."

"That is indicated, yes. Or..." Gawaine's voice died away. His eyes were unfocused, dreamily preoccupied.

David realised that one of the dons across the lawn was waving to them. He prodded Gawaine. "Isn't that the Dean?"

Gawaine returned abruptly to reality. "It is. And Porteus. I wonder what they want."

He led the way along the path to the edge of the lawn. As they approached, David had the bizarre impression of the Dean brandishing a sledge-hammer, and the thought crossed his mind that Verner might have slid irrevocably into a homicidal frenzy, before he identified the implement as a croquet mallet.

"Afternoon," the Dean greeted them. "We were just about to begin a game. Care to make a four?"

"I'm afraid I haven't played for years," Gawaine demurred.

"I haven't played at all," David added.

Useless. If anything, the Dean's enthusiasm increased. "Excellent! We'll teach you. Porteus, you and I had better split up."

"Then you take the novice, Dean," Porteus said thinly.

David was surprised that he should be there at all. Porteus did not strike him as a games-playing person. It was also the first time David had set eyes on him when he wasn't in a filthy temper. He still looked sour, but he wasn't overtly out for blood. At least, David reflected with some relief, he was not to have the honour of partnering him.

"Now look," the Dean began. "The object of the game is to drive your ball through each of these hoops in turn, and then hit that peg." He gestured with the mallet. "At the same time, of course, preventing your opponent from doing the same."

"You need to be devious, nasty and totally unscrupulous," Gawaine interposed.

"Should have thought that would come easy to you, in your line of work," Verner added.

Overwhelmed, David accepted a mallet and attempted to copy Gawaine, who was making a couple of practice swings. The Dean measured the distance from the first hoop and struck his ball smartly through. As Gawaine prepared to follow, David resigned himself to an hour of alternate boredom and humiliation.

In the event, it was not so bad. He had a fair eye for a ball, as befitted someone who played squash twice weekly with a fellow executive from the hellpit where both worked. Now he found that although croquet was not as physically demanding as squash, intellectually it had it beat, and he began to apply himself to the strategy.

"You know, you could be quite good," the Dean pronounced. They were progressing along the top of the lawn, slightly behind the other pair. He pointed to Gawaine's ball. "Think you can hit that?"

"Why not?"

David swung. The ball ran true across the turf and trickled to a stop a couple of inches short.

"Never mind, my dear David," Gawaine said sweetly. "Perhaps you would do better with a flamingo."

On that occasion, it was the Dean who got them out of trouble. He was, David began to realise, a very good player, probably the best of the four, though Porteus was almost as good, and Gawaine, to David's surprise, was proving quite competent.

"Have you been playing long, sir?" David asked the Dean during a moment's respite while their opponents discussed tactics. Verner had taken the opportunity to stuff his pipe with vile black tobacco, and lit up while he assessed the state of play.

The 'sir' got David a twitch of a shaggy eyebrow. "Long enough," the Dean replied. "My father taught me."

"Your father?" David inquired, almost on a reflex. What was it Gawaine had been saying about somebody's father?

"He was a damn' good player." Verner sucked deeply on his pipe. "Better than I am now. Tournament standard. They used to call him Sneaky Jack."

David's brain, suddenly going into overdrive, produced the memory of what Gawaine had said about somebody's father. "How interesting," he responded politely.

His next ball was nicely positioned for the next hoop. Porteus was aiming for it: a long shot.

"Not in a million years."

The balls kissed neatly. On his next shot, Porteus sent David's ball past the hoop, while placing his own just in front of it. Then he drove his ball through, with a faint hiss of satisfaction as it glanced off David's for a second time. A moment later, David was following his ball into the middle distance.

"Bloody hell," grunted the Dean.

Gawaine had mixed feelings about partnering Porteus. He had never, as an undergraduate, been on matey terms with his tutor. In fact he doubted that anyone, ever, had been matey with Porteus. He had always been remote, focused on the work and with no apparent interest in the personalities of any of his students. Now, with two murders to investigate, Gawaine knew he ought to slip in a few adroit questions, such as what had Porteus been doing on the morning Templeman was killed, but he found it very difficult to raise the subject tactfully.

"I remember playing croquet with Dr Templeman," he remarked.

Porteus was sizing up the position. "Oh, yes?" he said indifferently, not looking up.

He certainly did not gasp and quiver at the mention of his putative victim's name, but then, Gawaine wondered, did murderers ever? Probably as often as corpses spouted blood in their murderer's presence.

These were undoubtedly morbid thoughts for a July afternoon. Much pleasanter to enjoy the breeze in the lime trees and the Machiavellian pleasures of croquet.

"Did Dr Templeman still play?"

"What? Templeman? Oh, yes. I played with him last week."

"Thrashed you good and proper," the Dean commented, stumping past in pursuit of an errant ball.

Porteus smiled without humour. “Indeed.” He gestured to Gawaine. “Your turn.”

There was nothing much for Gawaine to do but drive his own ball closer to the hoop, which he did. There was a hiatus while the Dean gestured with his pipe to demonstrate David’s available options, and Gawaine meditated an unobtrusive way of asking Porteus where he had been on the previous Monday morning.

“Has it ever occurred to you,” Porteus began after a while, “how this croquet lawn could form an accurate metaphor for the world?” Not waiting for a reply – which would undoubtedly have been in the negative – he proceeded, “We all pursue our ambitions, as we attempt to pass through each successive hoop, in striving towards our ultimate objective, hitting the peg. In the process we are to some extent thwarted by our opponents, or by bad luck, if our ball should strike some unexpected irregularity, or by our own incompetence. Only the fittest win through.”

Gawaine was not sure how seriously to take him. “As a model of the universe,” he responded lightly, “it seems to lack a place for God. Unless of course you envisage the college gardener, who rolls the lawn and places the hoops in position…”

By no means,” Porteus interrupted. He was icy – not at all playful, as Gawaine belatedly realised. “No intelligent man, looking around him, can retain a belief in a beneficent Providence. This is the world of the antique gods, St Clair, about whom even you should retain a few stray memories. Harsh, cruel, irrational, and there are no second chances.”

He saw that David had finished his manoeuvre and

strode away to review the situation, leaving Gawaine feeling slightly chilled, and more than slightly bewildered.

"Not bad," the Dean grunted, peering benignly at his partner. "Not bad at all."

David basked.

"By the way," Verner went on," has St Clair come to any conclusions yet?"

It took David a few seconds to realise that they were back on the subject of the murders. "Not that I know of," he replied cautiously. He realised it was not the time to start chattering about reprints, letters, or Templeman's long-ago request for spiritual guidance.

"Expected to have you round, asking about my movements on Monday morning. Or doesn't St Clair work that way?"

Since if Gawaine had a method of working, David had failed to deduce what it was, he made nothing but a few appropriate noises in reply, but could not resist adding, "As you raised the matter, sir, what were your movements on Monday morning?"

What might have been a blast of anger came out as a chuckle. "Walked into that one, didn't I?" Verner thrust a hand through his thatch of white hair. "And no, I haven't a watertight alibi. In the early part of the morning I was in my room, working, until I was dragged into coping with those infernal bones – calling the police, holding the Master's hand, and so on and so forth. Then after about eleven thirty I was back in my room, working again. Correction. Trying to work. I had one short visit from the Master, and then I phoned St Clair. But apart from that – no, pity, but I had plenty of time to kill Templeman."

That was candid, David thought, as the Dean walked off to take his turn. But then, if he was guilty, it would pay him to be candid. There was nothing definite to be deduced from what he had just said, but it was an additional piece of information to be passed on to Gawaine afterwards.

Gawaine had his mind occupied for some time by a tricky little manoeuvre that got him through the last but one hoop. When he had finished, successfully, he found Porteus at his elbow again. "What are you doing these days?" he asked abruptly.

Gawaine shrugged. "Oh, this and that," he replied, deliberately vague.

"You never think about coming back?"

That was a surprise. Porteus had never made any secret of the fact that he had watched Gawaine's departure with no regret whatsoever.

"No, I never do," Gawaine replied. "I'm afraid I assume that all that is over and done with."

"Not necessarily. If you decided that you wanted to finish your degree, I don't believe anyone in College would stand in your way."

Gawaine considered. He did not sound friendly – Porteus never sounded friendly – but the statement was in some way designed to be an olive branch. Shying away from anything that might commit him later, he replied, "Thank you – but I don't believe it's possible."

"You prefer your current pastime of hunting murderers?" The venom was back in Porteus's voice, the olive branch swiftly retracted and claws extended in its place.

"Scarcely 'prefer,'" Gawaine murmured in response.

"It seems a strange way to choose to spend your time. Why do you do it? The publicity?"

Suddenly Gawaine found himself on the defensive. The last thing he felt like doing was justifying himself to Porteus, especially in the middle of a game of croquet. With the languid manner that he found so useful in circumstances like these, he began, "Really, Dr Porteus, I scarcely imagine that – "

"I will not be questioned," Porteus interrupted. "You may be here at the Dean's request, but you have no official standing. I will carry out my obligations to the police, but beyond that I will not be questioned. Do I make myself clear?"

"Admirably."

Just as well, Gawaine reflected, that he had not started to frame any tactful references to what Porteus was doing on Monday morning. Any such attempt might have ended in his being attacked with a mallet. He consoled himself by thinking that he could probably extract the information from Inspector Carter. Its accuracy would be suspect in any case, unless Porteus had mentioned the reprint. All in all, it had been an odd conversation. Definitely illogical. And not, he thought, the conversation of a double murderer. At least…

Gawaine's musings were brought to a close by the thwack of the Dean's ball as it collided smartly with the peg. Pulling himself together, he tried to concentrate on the fag-end of the game.

"Well," the Dean said, still crusty, but triumphant at a narrowly snatched victory. "For a first try, you could have done a good deal worse." The look he was giving David suggested that he might be prepared to consider the admission of advertising executives to civilised society. "Tea, Porteus?"

"No, thank you, Dean." Porteus's tones were brusque, just this side of rudeness. "I've work to do. I've wasted too much time already." He stalked off.

The Dean watched him out of sight. "Poor loser," he grunted. "Always did want the penny and the bun. Never mind." He gestured expansively with his mallet. "Tea?"

Chapter Fifteen

'In Philosophy, where Truth seems double-fac'd, there is no man more Paradoxical than myself.'

Religio Medici

"Sneaky Jack? The Dean's father was known as Sneaky Jack?"

David nodded. "So he said."

"My dear David, I'm overwhelmed!" Gawaine's eyes were brilliant with approval. "Such perspicacity. I have clearly been underestimating you."

David preened.

"And Jack is, of course, 'a notorious domesticity for John'. Mmm…"

They were leaving Dr Verner's rooms after a further cup of tea, this time scalding hot and strong enough to crawl out of the pot unassisted. David was beginning to feel the need for something stronger still.

"Though John is, of course, a fairly common name," Gawaine continued reflectively. "Let's put this on an official footing. I'm going to phone Carter." He slid out his mobile phone, but before he could ring the number they were interrupted by the appearance of Inspector Carter himself, heading into college through the lodge with a crisply dressed woman sergeant at his heels.

"Inspector!" Gawaine greeted him. "How delightful. We were just about to phone you."

"I'm glad I've caught you," Carter replied, refraining from asking what the call would have been about. "I've come to take some fingerprints, and I shall need yours for elimination."

"Fingerprints?" Gawaine frowned in a puzzled fashion as he turned back towards the college buildings. "Of course, Inspector, but – " He came to a dead stop on the threshold. "You've found fingerprints on that letter?"

Inspector Carter took him firmly by the elbow and propelled him inside. "Suppose we don't tell the whole of the College about it?" he suggested mildly.

Still thoroughly agitated, Gawaine managed to repress further speech until the four of them were in his room with the door closed. David thought that if he offered to provide yet another cup of tea he would stage a personal rebellion, but nothing seemed further from Gawaine's mind. He paced fretfully while the sergeant got out her scanner and Carter lectured on the subject of recovering prints after such a long time.

"The letter was protected of course, or we might never have managed it. There are two sets of recent prints on the edges – those must be yours. And closer to the centre, traces that must be Templeman's and the girl's, and one very nice, unidentified, grimy thumb print."

"Which is all you need! Inspector, the person who handled that letter must be the father of Sue's baby, and it must have been the same person who murdered Templeman, and so – " Gawaine broke off, looking slightly sick, and then made one attempt to rally. "So, in that case,

Inspector..." His voice trailed away and he pretended a fascinated interest in the sergeant's operations as she fingerprinted David.

"In that case," Carter agreed, "we could be onto a good thing. What was it you wanted to talk to me about?"

Gawaine launched into a dissertation on the subject of little boys and their grandfathers, and the name of John.

Carter looked thoughtful. "We may not need it," he commented, "but it's an idea."

"It's somewhat embarrassing," Gawaine remarked, with a nervous look at the sergeant as she ran the scanner over his fingertips, as if he expected the device to explode, "to go round asking people what their father was called. Rather obvious. You, Inspector, will find it much easier to go to the official records – though David," he added with a nod to his friend, "managed to discover that Dr Verner's father was John. That should get you started."

"Porteus's name is John," Carter told them. "His second name. Miles John."

Gawaine's brows rose. "Really? Fascinating."

David was aware of an edginess about him that he had not really expected, now that they were drawing so close to the solution of the problem. Gawaine ought to have been relieved...but then, he was never all that happy about the moment when the trap finally closed. Especially if it closed around the Dean or the Chaplain, whom he clearly liked, or round Porteus, for whom he obviously held a much more complicated set of feelings, or the Bursar, whose family life he had admired. Better if it was Heatherington, David reflected, not really thinking that it could be.

Chiming exactly on his thought, Inspector Carter said, "By the way, we've managed to eliminate at least one suspect for Templeman's murder."

"Oh, really?" Gawaine asked. "Whom?"

"Heatherington. He has an alibi."

Now in a detective story, David thought, it would really be Heatherington. Beware the unbreakable alibi. But as they were experiencing what passed these days for real life, it probably meant that he was definitely eliminated. Pity. David had not fancied what he had seen of Heatherington at all.

Meanwhile Inspector Carter was elaborating on Heatherington's alibi. "From nine until twelve, he was on duty in the porter's lodge. Templeman was having his breakfast at nine, and I suspect that he was dead by twelve. In any case, when Simpson relieved Heatherington at twelve o'clock, he left the college. At ten past twelve he was buying cigarettes in his local corner shop, and at twelve fifteen he was entering his own house and about to eat the lunch lovingly prepared by the hands of Mrs Heatherington. He was seen there at about twelve-thirty by their next door neighbour who popped over for a chat and stayed until nearly one. After that – well, Heatherington wasn't due back in college until three, and Templeman was definitely dead by one o'clock, when he failed to turn up to lunch with Marcia Scott."

David looked at that. He was developing a nose, he thought, for loopholes in alibis, but Heatherington's seemed altogether too watertight. It made him uneasy.

"Can you be sure he was in the lodge for the whole three hours?" he asked the Inspector.

Carter shrugged. "Sure enough. Several of the dons looked in for their mail. We've tracked down a couple of visitors to college who saw him there. And he was on the switchboard to deal with phone calls. Besides, we haven't managed to find a single person who saw him anywhere else in that time." He paused, his gaze reflective and inward-looking. "And that reminds me," he went on. "You can forget about Marcia Scott. She was definitely at Lady Margaret Hall on Monday at lunch time. Several people corroborate that. And we haven't found anyone who admits seeing her in college on Monday morning."

Gawaine gave David a look of relief. "I was sure Marcia Scott was telling the truth." Sitting down again, he frowned thoughtfully. "Heatherington must have known about the bones," he began, as if feeling his way. "He would have dealt with the phone call to the police, and I'm positive, Inspector, knowing Heatherington, that he would have listened in. So he could have realised the... the expediency of murdering Templeman. He could even have slipped away from the lodge for ten minutes to do it. But he couldn't rely on doing it and not being missed. It would have been too much of a risk. One thing's funny, though..." He paused.

"Enlighten us," David suggested.

"All this...kerfuffle. Bones. Police. Dons panicking all over the place. And Heatherington quietly strolls out of college and returns to the bosom of his family?"

"Perhaps he didn't want to be involved," Carter said.

Gawaine shook his head impatiently. "Not Heatherington. A frightfully nosy character, Inspector, always up with the latest gossip. He has an intelligence network all over the College, and there isn't much that he doesn't know about. His natural reaction should have been to go and see for himself what it was all about."

David saw that the Inspector, who had been listening to Gawaine ramble on with an expression of good-humoured tolerance, suddenly looked more interested. "Odd," he said. "Yes, definitely odd. When someone steps out of character like that, you look for a reason."

"Maybe Mrs Heatherington belts him with a rolling pin if he's late for lunch," David suggested.

Gawaine gave him a pained, flickering glance, but said nothing.

"Still," Carter continued, "whatever the reason is, he can't have killed Templeman. That alibi holds."

David felt that if he had his way it would not hold for long, but he had to admit that he could see no way of breaking it. The man had been on duty. He had then left. And afterwards he was accounted for. That, for the moment, was that. At least their other four suspects had alibis that were not watertight, and the fingerprint on the letter should soon tell them which one was guilty.

"What about the Bursar?" Gawaine asked nervily. "Have you checked his alibi?"

Carter shrugged. "We can't find anyone who saw him in college that morning. And we questioned Mrs Morrison again. Nothing new. She stands by what she said. He was in bed with a stomach upset. If we believe her, he has an alibi, but…well, she is his wife."

"And because she's his wife she must be lying to protect him?" Gawaine queried, a fretful note in his voice.

"Would you prefer her if she shopped him?" Carter retorted.

Gawaine consigned the point to oblivion with an expressive wave of the hand. "And Porteus?" he asked, adding almost immediately, "If you don't mind, Inspector. He won't talk to me."

"Nothing." Carter seemed quite amenable to questioning, unlike the subject of their conversation. "He says he spent the whole morning working in his room, and didn't find out about the bones until he came down to lunch. He also says that he didn't see Templeman all that morning. No way of checking that, but it could be true."

Gawaine, of course, was in possession of evidence that Porteus was lying. David waited, interested to see if he would divulge it. But he said nothing. It seemed hardly friendly, when Carter was being so obliging, but David knew that Gawaine still felt, for what reason he couldn't imagine, some sort of compulsion to protect Porteus from police interest. David wondered how Carter would react if he ever found out.

Meanwhile Carter's sergeant had put away her scanner, and the Inspector took his leave. "If you want to know about this," he said to Gawaine, "you'd better drop into the station, or phone from a mobile. I'm beginning to get the idea that it's just as well not to talk on the college phones. Heatherington." He grinned ruefully. "And they talk about police wire-tapping!"

"Are you going to make an arrest?" Gawaine asked nervously.

Carter gave him a long look. "Not quite yet. You'll be warned."

He left. Gawaine remained in silence, staring at the door.

"Well?" David asked. "Whose fingerprint? A one in five chance. Do you want to make a bet?"

Gawaine gave him a look of fastidious distaste. "Don't."

"I'd go for the Chaplain myself."

The look dissolved into a faint, reluctant smile. "I thought your money was on Porteus." He ran a hand through his hair. "I must admit, the state of my current thinking…"

"You think it's Porteus?"

"Something about that letter did occur to me, but – no, it's probably nothing. The fingerprint will tell us, in any case. Of course," he added, "were this a detective story, now that Heatherington has been eliminated conclusively for the murder of Templeman, the fingerprint on the letter would naturally be his."

"Rubbish!"

David had cause to remember that remark later. When he phoned Inspector Carter for the information, the fingerprint did indeed prove to be Heatherington's.

Chapter Sixteen

'Things cannot get out of their natures, or be or not be in spite of their constitutions.'
Christian Morals, III.xxiii

"Heatherington!" If you could hiss a name totally lacking in sibilants, David would have hissed it. "It can't be Heatherington!"

"Tell that to forensics." Inspector Carter's voice, coming through David's mobile, was totally dead-pan. "Keep in touch." He rang off.

David put his phone away and reported the conversation to Gawaine. For privacy, they were sitting in David's car, parked in the lane outside the college. "But Heatherington has an alibi for Templeman's murder," he finished.

"I know." Gawaine's eyes were sparkling. "Isn't it perfectly delightful?"

He was, David recognised, looking a great deal happier than before. A substantial part of him had not wanted an arrest. And now that the net, instead of closing in, had gone back to square one... Even David recognised a certain confusion of thought. *And why not, when everything's confused*?

"It seems we have two options," Gawaine continued,

getting out of the car and heading for the college gate. "Abandon the assumption that the fingerprint belongs to the father of Sue's baby, or – "

"Or break Heatherington's alibi!" David locked the car and followed. "I never did like that alibi. It's far too neat. Look here –" He broke off momentarily as they passed through the lodge, where a younger porter, presumably Simpson, was on duty. "Your friend Templeman couldn't have been the father himself?"

"No – or who murdered him?"

"Right. Yet the father's fingerprints must be on the letter, because it was sent to him. Right?"

"That is very true, Socrates."

David considered following that diversion, then decided to ignore it. "And the only other set of fingerprints was Heatherington's. Therefore he was the father. Therefore he killed Sue and Templeman. All we have to do is prove it."

There was no response from Gawaine other than a deep sigh. He led David through a passageway into a cloister, part of the college David had not visited before. For a while they leant on the cloister wall in companiable silence.

"I should like to know," Gawaine remarked eventually, "how Templeman's prints came to be on that letter."

"He gave it to what's-her-name…"

"Marcia Scott. Quite. But how did he come to have it in the first place?"

"He wasn't the type to go around reading other people's letters?" David asked.

"Emphatically not."

David, not having known Templeman, thought himself justified in not accepting Gawaine's certainty. "You know what occurs to me?"

Gawaine turned an inquiring look on him.

"This business – keeping a letter, not a letter that belonged to him personally, for years, keeping it in a safe place…come on, Gawaine, what does that suggest to you?"

He was gratified, and at the same time conscience-stricken, to see that Gawaine had gone quite white.

"Nothing, my dear David, will ever make me believe that Templeman went in for blackmail." In the face of David's scepticism, he added more forcefully, "He couldn't. It just wasn't in him."

David made himself ignore his friend's distress. "No? It fits, you have to admit that. He blackmailed Heatherington with that letter, and Heatherington killed him."

As he spoke, Gawaine's shocked look faded, and was replaced with a puzzled expression. "After thirty years? He put up with blackmail for thirty years, and then killed him on the very morning the girl's body was discovered?"

"Because he was frightened of what Templeman knew. He thought it was all going to come out."

Gawaine shook his head, more in bewilderment than denial, and said no more. David wondered how much of that he was prepared to accept, and how much he rejected because of what he knew, or thought he knew, about Templeman. He had spent too long, in David's view, groping around and ignoring the facts if they didn't happen to agree with his personal feelings. To David himself, the theory hung together nicely, and not just because it was his own theory. He wondered what Inspector Carter would think of it. It should be possible, he thought, to check bank accounts, any unusual expenditure...all the things the police were so good at, that he and Gawaine could not do at all.

Somewhere, not far away, a bell had begun to toll rhythmically.

"We could go and ask some questions," David suggested. "See the tobacconist, maybe Heatherington's wife, and the next door neighbour."

"What for – oh, the alibi!"

"Yes, the alibi. Or even better, ask around College and try to find some evidence that Heatherington wasn't on duty when he was supposed to be. That's when he must have done it." He realised that he had less than his friend's full attention. Gawaine was still leaning on the cloister wall, gazing pensively across a stretch of exceptionally boring lawn. "Couldn't we?" David persisted.

Gawaine came to himself with a slight shudder. "Of course we could, my dear David, but what good do you think it would do? The police are very efficient at that sort of thing, and they're bound to have another look at it now."

David was beginning to feel annoyed. "So you won't?"

"No."

"Why – because you'd rather let a murderer escape than have any muck-raking about Templeman...what is that bloody bell?"

"Chapel." Gawaine glanced at his watch. "Five minutes. Evensong."

"But it's Thursday."

Gawaine gave him a look that would have stripped paint.

"All right, it's Thursday," David said hastily. "See if I care. What are you going to do?"

"Do?" Gawaine detached himself from the cloister wall and brushed himself down with some care. "I shall go to Chapel. Coming?"

"No, thanks."

Gawaine turned away, then swung back. David could not read his expression; he had an odd, quirky smile. "Dinner afterwards?"

David nodded. "Sure."

Gawaine disappeared down the cloister. A moment later, the bell stopped. In the silence, David wondered if he had been close to that unprecedented situation, a quarrel with Gawaine. His own fault, if so. He didn't give a damn who had murdered or been murdered, blackmailed or anything else – but Gawaine cared, desperately, and it was beginning to look as if he couldn't go on championing Sue and Templeman at one and the same time. And David had a good idea of where that was going to lead. Send not, he thought, recalling something that Gawaine was fond of quoting, to ask for whom the bell tolls; it tolls, worse luck, for thee.

Gawaine slipped into a pew near the back of the chapel just before the bell stopped and Father Gerard, suddenly dignified in priest's robes, paced into the sanctuary. The service proceeded: hymns, readings, prayers. No sermon. The choir, rather depleted out of term, sang Palestrina. Gawaine himself had sung in the choir, read the lesson. A long time ago. Candlelight on polished wood, velvet, carved angels soaring out of stone. Outside the day had grown overcast, and the colours slept in the stained glass.

Lighten our darkness… Templeman a blackmailer? Not if anything made sense. 'If there is rule in unity itself…'

And yet there was that letter. And David's suggestions had made an uncomfortable sort of sense. It wasn't possible just to push it away. It was there, and he would have no peace until he accounted for it. 'The peace of God that passeth all understanding…' Not here. Not yet.

The service over, the small congregation filed out. Gawaine stayed where he was. He was mildly surprised to see Heatherington among those present, and automatically looked round for the Dean, Porteus and the Bursar, but none of them was there. It would have been too much to expect all five suspects to present themselves for Chapel, though it would have been neat.

Heatherington, now he supposed elevated to the position of chief suspect, looked smugly pleased with himself. The afternoon's fingerprinting ceremony could not have aroused his suspicions. If he was being blackmailed, if he knew of the existence of that letter, ought he to have been suspicious?

Gawaine's train of thought was interrupted as the Chaplain, once more in his shabby black cassock, sat down beside him.

"My dear fellow."

Gawaine found it hard to meet his eyes. "I'm making a mess of this."

"Surely not."

"I thought I knew, Father. At least, things were… beginning to make sense. But now…"

Father Gerard was watching him shrewdly over the top of his half-moon spectacles. "Something else has occurred? Possibly connected with the fact that the police took several sets of fingerprints this afternoon?"

Gawaine was not sure how to reply to that. Father Gerard's guesses were coming uncomfortably close.

"Don't worry, my dear fellow," the Chaplain continued. "Say no more than you must. I am, of course, aware that I must come under suspicion."

Something about his voice – the level tones with a world of tolerance and even humour – made Gawaine feel thoroughly ashamed of himself. He kept his eyes fixed on the prayer book, reposing on a fat velvet cushion in front of him. "I shouldn't be here," he said.

"No? I've always found this – " he made a little gesture, and Gawaine was not sure whether he meant the chapel, or the college, or even Oxford itself – "to be an extremely accommodating place."

"All the same, I'm supposed to be representing the College's interest, and I'm making a mess of it. Even David thinks so."

"David? Ah, yes, your friend. An extremely level-headed young man, if I may say so. I suggest you listen to him."

Gawaine half-smiled. "If I did, Father, I might cause a good deal of unpleasantness."

"The College can stand any amount of unpleasantness," the Chaplain replied, surprising Gawaine by his robust tones. "What we can't stand is this uncertainty. We look around us at people we've worked with for years – not always seen eye to eye with, naturally, but people we thought we knew – and we ask ourselves, 'Was it you?' Put a stop to that, Gawaine, and we'll forgive you any amount of unpleasantness."

"Not all of you."

"You mean the one who did it? Oh, yes. After thirty years? Don't you think that after all that time he's only looking for a chance to shed the burden?" Father Gerard got to his feet, and his voice was bleak. "That's important, my dear fellow. Nothing else."

When he had gone, silence settled around Gawaine. The server had long since extinguished the candles. The main lights went out, leaving only the glow of the sanctuary lamp. Gawaine bowed his head. He tried to suppress himself, his own fears and wishes, and put himself at the service of the truth, even the uncompromising truth that Father Gerard had outlined. He reached out with his mind, not across distance, but through time, to meet Sue as she arrived in Oxford, thirty years ago.

She had come from a distance, for the Oxford police had found no suitable missing person locally. And she had come…by train. Probably by train. And from the station – a taxi, because she wouldn't know about the local buses, and if she was six months pregnant she wouldn't want to walk. But you couldn't trace a taxi after thirty years, could you? And the taxi had put her off at the college gates, been paid and driven away, and there Sue was, not looking for revenge, not out to make trouble, just happy because she was going to see her baby's father, so she would go…

Gawaine suddenly sat up. He had been, he reflected, incredibly stupid. It was not much consolation that everyone else had been incredibly stupid as well. He was so involved with his new idea that he did not hear the door of the chapel softly open, and then, just as softly, close.

Chapter Seventeen

'...the long habit of living indisposeth us for dying...'
Urne Buriall, Ch 5

David went back to his room, showered in a bathroom of creaking antiquity, and changed. While he did so, he played with the idea of phoning Inspector Carter again, and suggesting that he should investigate the bank accounts of Templeman and Heatherington. And perhaps some of the others for good measure. The more he thought about it, the more he liked it, but he knew that he would do no such thing, if only because he could not face the thought of admitting it to Gawaine afterwards.

He was not sure whether Gawaine had gone to Chapel to escape the theory, purely to annoy, or out of a genuine need for spiritual support. Knowing Gawaine, it could be any of those reasons, if not all. David resolutely refused to analyse the problem. Whatever Gawaine's motives, he was welcome to them; only, David thought when he had finished dressing, it was taking him an unreasonably long time.

He left his room again, intending to lurk outside the chapel until the service was over. Entering the cloister, he almost cannoned into the Dean, stumping along with his hands in the pockets of his shapeless tweed jacket.

"Looking for you," Verner announced ominously.

David wondered why his stock had suddenly risen. An aptitude for croquet, perhaps? "Anything I can do…" he murmured.

"Damn' all," Verner retorted, which was at least reassuring in that it restored the *status quo*. "Just tell me where I can find St Clair."

"In the chapel."

"What's he doing there?"

Without waiting for an answer, the Dean reversed smartly and began striding along the cloister. David kept pace with him. Verner seemed to think that he had to make conversation, for after a few seconds he barked out, "Your first time in Oxford?"

"Yes."

"Must think we're a load of loonies."

That was so self-evident that David made no reply.

"They must do things differently at – where? Essex? LSE?"

"Keele, sir. Business Management."

Verner came to a halt as they approached the doors of the chapel and peered at David with the scepticism of a man encountering for the first time a member of a race in which he has, so far, refused to believe. David stood his ground. He had not been born erudite, he had failed to achieve erudition, and he was damned if he was going to have erudition thrust upon him at this late stage. He had taken a practical course, and achieved exactly what he had set out to achieve.

After a moment Verner snorted and abandoned his glare. "Could be a good choice," he admitted. "We never did St Clair much good."

"What did you do, sack him?" David couldn't resist the question.

"We don't 'sack' undergraduates, young man," the Dean informed him testily. "We send them down. Though not in St Clair's case."

"Then what the hell happened?"

"He hasn't told you?"

"No."

The Dean paused. David had time to wonder if he was going to answer, and then whether he wanted him to answer.

Verner was frowning. "Porteus was his tutor," he said slowly. "The undergraduates have a saying about Porteus. All his students either end up getting a First, or having a nervous breakdown." He paused again, then added, "I should have thought myself St Clair was a certain First."

David said nothing, although what the Dean had told him made sense of a great deal. It certainly explained Gawaine's equivocal attitude to Porteus, and why he had been so apprehensive about visiting Oxford again.

What it did not make sense of was why Gawaine should agree to return to the College, for any reason, and particularly to ease the dons over a rough patch. But then, Gawaine was Gawaine. David found a renewed satisfaction in contemplating Porteus as a possible murderer.

"He still could, you know," the Dean went on abruptly.

"Could what?"

"Finish his degree."

For some reason David felt a spurt of anger. "Why should he want to do that?"

"Don't just dismiss it," Verner said, fishing in his

pocket for his pipe. “I know he has no practical use for a degree. But it’s failure. Unfinished business. He won’t be right until he comes back to face it. You could persuade him.”

“I can’t think of any reason why I should want to try.” Forestalling any reply the Dean might have made, he turned away and faced the door of the chapel. “Long services you have around here.”

The Dean was at his side, the pipe evidently forgotten. “Not as long as this.”

There was, of course, no reason for it, but David felt a cold movement of uneasiness in the pit of his stomach. All nonsense; Gawaine could be anywhere. Then why didn’t he come to find me first? Only one reason: there might be danger in what he was doing. No, he was probably gossiping over a cup of tea with Father Gerard.

The Dean pushed open a heavy door which led into a small foyer. Everything was dark. An inner door led into the chapel itself, lit by a single lamp at the far end. Verner took a step or two inside, footsteps echoing. David followed. The building held a quietness that was not simply an absence of sound. The subdued light showed fluted columns and arches soaring into darkness, the ranks of pews, and, like a rock in a smooth river, a dark shape huddled in the centre aisle.

David started forward. Gawaine was lying face down, half in and half out of the pew. He was still. The short haft of a knife stuck out from one side. David reached for it.

“Don’t touch it!” the Dean snapped.

He whirled and was gone. David was hardly aware of him, but he checked the movement and stood rigid, staring down. Briefly he closed his eyes. If he sent out all his will, this would prove to be madness, for there was no believing it. But when he opened his eyes, the body still lay there.

Moving nothing but his head, he looked around, for it occurred to him that the murderer might still be there. He wished he could be, for then there would be something he could do. But he saw nothing, except another image of torment in the crucifix above the pulpit. Gawaine had believed in that, he knew, but what was the use of it, when this could happen, here?

He looked down again, and this time he saw the truth. It was over. Never again. He had never asked himself how much it had meant, until now.

"No," he said aloud. "Gawaine. No."

There was a whisper of movement at his feet. The fingers of one hand uncurled, groped feebly outwards, and were still. And he heard his name, breathed into the silence.

"David."

By then he was on his knees, gripping the hand that had moved, and then fumbling to find the pulse. He could hear each shallow breath, very faint, irregular, so that in the pause between each one he thought there would never be another.

Footsteps sounded, approached from the door: Verner. David looked up at him. "He's not dead," he said, as if he was announcing a tragedy.

And not long after that there were police, and ambulance men, and eventually a hospital, clinical and anonymous, where Gawaine was whisked away, and David found himself in a waiting room, facing the Dean.

He had nothing to say to him. Someone had tried to kill Gawaine; David still did not know if they had succeeded. And the Dean had been there, hurrying away from the chapel when he met David. The tale about looking for Gawaine could have been a blind. And the others? Father Gerard must be a possibility. David tried to give his mind to opportunity so that he could distract it from what was going on elsewhere in the hospital, and failed totally.

Not long after, Father Gerard arrived, quietly and without explanation, and sat down to wait with them. He seemed drawn into himself, his eyes unfocused, and David realised he must be praying. He felt briefly envious that he himself had no such certainty; even while he doubted that it would make any difference, it was somehow comforting. His own mind was like a dark room with someone flashing up slides on a screen: odd memories of Gawaine, scraps that he thought he had forgotten, but especially, again and again, that quizzical look Gawaine had given him before he went off down the cloister to the chapel.

He was never sure how long they sat there, not speaking. At last the door opened. A nurse stood there, surveying the three of them impersonally.

"Is one of you called David?" she asked.

Chapter Eighteen

'I never yet cast a true affection on a woman; but I have loved my friend as I do virtue, my soul, my God.'
Religio Medici

David got to his feet. The nurse beckoned him and he followed her out into the corridor. "Is he – ?" he started to ask, and broke off.

He could not think exactly how he wanted to phrase the question; there should be some way of doing it that would give him the answer he wanted.

The nurse gave him an unexpectedly warm smile. "He's not going to die, if that's what you're asking," she replied. "He's been very lucky. The knife glanced off a rib and just tore muscle. Half an inch in the other direction, and we'd be having a very different conversation." She stopped outside another door and opened it. "You can have five minutes, no more."

As David entered the room, someone else was getting up from the chair beside the bed. David had never seen him before; he was a solid-looking young man dressed in plain clothes that still managed to shriek 'police'. He tucked away a notebook, and gave David a smile and a nod as he passed him on his way out.

David did not acknowledge it; he was too intent on

Gawaine. Somehow, even though he knew how close to death his friend had been, he had not expected him to look quite so white and fragile. He could think of nothing to say; any words that came into his head sounded impossibly trite. He took the vacated chair, and found that he had to take refuge in banality after all.

"How do you feel?"

Gawaine smiled faintly. His blue eyes were drowsy, as if he was drugged, but there was suddenly a spark of amusement there. "Perfectly foul," he murmured.

"Did you see anything?"

A slight shake of the head. "That's what Sergeant Drayton there was asking…sorry I can't help." A frown gathered between his brows. "I was thinking…thinking about Sue. I had an idea…" His voice trailed off, and then began again, stronger now, but alarming David because he had started to sound agitated. "I can't remember, David. It was important, and I can't remember."

"You will, soon. Don't work yourself up."

To his relief, Gawaine sighed and seemed to relax. "I'm sorry. I'm being a frightful nuisance… You look terrible."

David forced a smile, and consciously tried not to look terrible. "It was a shock, finding you there," he admitted.

"'No place indeed should murder sanctuarise…' A perfectly appalling line, don't you think, and if things had gone differently I should have made a point of telling him so…"

Gawaine's voice drifted into silence once more. David felt alarmed again; he was obviously rambling. He wondered if he ought to call someone, but before he could make his mind up, Gawaine said, "David, do something for me."

"Yes – what?"

"Get out of Oxford. Now. Tonight."

That was the last thing David had expected to hear him say. "I'm damned if I'll leave you here!" he protested, too loudly.

"Please, David. Someone tried to kill me. He thinks I know something, and if he thinks you know it too he might try…David, I can't stay here thinking about it, I can't take it, if – "

"Stop it," David interrupted. He was thoroughly frightened; Gawaine had reached across to clutch at his arm, and he was trying to sit up. "Stop it. Listen, for God's sake."

Gawaine was lying still again, more from lack of strength, David thought, than because he felt at all reassured. His hands were shaking.

David leant forward. "Listen. I can't go. Carter won't let me. There's Templeman's inquest tomorrow, don't forget. But I'll leave the college. I'll go straight back there now, pack up and go to a hotel. I'll be perfectly all right." *And very glad of an excuse to get out of the place*, he added mentally.

Gawaine, though he still looked shaken, had grown calmer, as if David's urgency had begun to convince him.

"You will be careful?"

"Yes, I will. I'll lock my door, and – oh hell."

The final muttered words were a response to the reappearance of the nurse, who surveyed the state Gawaine was in with tight-lipped disapproval. David got up; once again he did not know what to say.

Gawaine looked up at him with a ghost of his old, charming smile. "Don't forget, David. Take care."

"You too."

He got himself out into the corridor, and the nurse closed the door on him.

A few minutes later, when he felt he could face people again, David went back to the waiting-room. He was startled to see that the Dean and Chaplain had been joined by Seff Brown. She was sitting next to Father Gerard, speaking to him in an urgent undertone, and he was actually holding her hand, for all the world as if she were an ordinary weak and feeble woman in need of reassurance.

Seconds later the tableau broke up as the Dean realised David had come in and rose to his feet. "Well?"

"He's all right," David replied. "At least, he's not all right, but he will be."

"Thank God!" Father Gerard said, from the heart.

David had the awful feeling that for two pins Seff might cry.

"What are you doing here, looking for a story?" he asked.

As he had expected, the question brought Seff snapping back to normal. "It's my job, hadn't you noticed?" she retorted. Her voice lashed at him. "The modern resurrection man. As there isn't going to be a corpse, I'll be on my way." She stood up, grabbing her bag.

"My dear Miss Brown…" Father Gerard protested mildly.

"I'm sorry, Father. He gets on my nerves." She turned back to David. "I'm going back to my hotel, to write my story, and send it in like a good little ghoul. Unless you have any other comments to make?"

"Yes," David said, in the mood to provoke her. "If you've got your car here, you can give me a lift back to college."

In the end, still seething, Seff drove all three of them back to St Clement's. During the long wait in the hospital, David had lost all count of time, and when it occurred to him to look at his watch, he was surprised to see it was almost midnight.

The college gates were locked; Verner hunted for his keys and unfastened a small door set in the larger one. David explained to him why he would want to get out again later; the explanation was interrupted by Seff.

"David," she began, sounding as if, unwillingly, she might be displaying a flag of truce, "are you going to pack a case for Gawaine? I'll take it round to the hospital if you like."

David examined that for ulterior motive. "What about your story?"

"I can worry about that, thanks."

"Look here," Verner interrupted. "I can't stand here while you argue all night." He thrust a key into David's hand. "Take this, lock up after you, and drop it in some time tomorrow. I'm going to bed."

He stalked off. Father Gerard wished them good night and followed.

David and Seff were left looking at each other on the outside of the door. Then, without speaking, Seff stepped through into the college.

"Where do you think you're going?" David asked.

"I'll help you," Seff said innocently. "You do your own stuff, I'll pack Gawaine's. It's late."

David had no choice but to follow her. Throwing her out physically was beyond him; for one thing, he would never dare. And after all, he reflected, there was no reason to quarrel with her. She had her points. She had been upset about Gawaine, back there.

"You wouldn't have wanted to weep over everyone," he remarked.

"And just what do you mean by that?"

"Just that I might not be as nasty as you think."

There was a short pause. Then: "I do not weep," Seff said icily, but the words were followed by a faint grin in his direction. "I'll tell you what, David," she added a moment later, in what were, for her, surprisingly friendly tones. "When we've done this packing, you can buy me a meal. I know a Chinese place that stays open. I haven't eaten, and I'm pretty sure you haven't."

David had forgotten all about food. He had been planning dinner with Gawaine, in what seemed like another decade. He now realised that he was ravenous - and a stiff drink would do no harm, either. "Okay," he agreed.

He left Seff outside Gawaine's room while he went on to his own. Packing his case did not take long. He wondered where he was likely to find a hotel room at this time, but pushed the problem out of his mind. He had promised Gawaine not to spend the night in college, and he intended to stand by that. If all else failed, he could go to Carter and ask for the protection of a cell.

He returned to find Seff in Gawaine's sitting room. Gawaine's case was ready by the door. Seff herself was standing by the waste paper bin, looking down into it with a thoughtful expression.

"What's the matter?" David asked.

"The scout hasn't emptied the bin. The rooms have been done, but the bin hasn't been emptied since yesterday."

"Civilisation will crumble," David said, preoccupied by thoughts of prawn foo yung. "Get a move on."

Seff did not move. "Civilisation will crumble," she rejoined, "on the day Oxford scouts stop emptying bins."

"So what?" David asked impatiently.

"So do you remember what's in this bin?"

This time David contented himself with an elaborately heavy sigh.

"Listen, idiot," Seff said. "Or rather, look. What do you see in there?"

Realising when he was defeated, David put down his own case and joined her. There was nothing in the bin except for the notes that Seff had made for the news story she had written the day before. David remembered Gawaine throwing them in there after Seff had left.

"So?"

"How Gawaine puts up with it, I'll never know," Seff muttered. "Listen. I wrote that, and put that bit at the end that Gawaine dictated, about having evidence that would lead to the father of the baby. A direct invitation for someone to murder him. And now someone has – or did their best to."

"You think someone saw? But..."

David's protest died away. The door had not been locked. The notes were not even in shorthand, but in Seff's own brand of speedwriting, that was perfectly legible, with a bit of effort. David could see that what he had warned Gawaine about could easily have happened; it was no consolation at all to be proved right.

"Wouldn't he have taken the notes away?" he wondered aloud.

"He might have thought it was safer to leave them. If he was trying to be a little bit clever."

"Then why didn't the scout take them?"

"Maybe because he was in here doing the scout's job. A good excuse for a nose round, wouldn't you say?"

David saw the light. "Heatherington!"

"Check. Any of them could have come in to search, but only Heatherington had a legitimate reason for being here."

Seff knelt by the bin, unzipped a section of her bag, and taking each sheet of her notes delicately by one corner, she dropped them in.

"I might be making a fuss about nothing," she said, "but I'm taking those to Inspector Carter tomorrow, to have them fingerprinted."

"What is it with you and Gawaine?" Seff Brown asked, neatly capturing a sliver of chicken between her chopsticks. "I could understand it if you were gay, but I know you're not, either of you. You're just…weird."

"Thank you for that insight," David muttered.

He gazed around the restaurant, taking in the flock wallpaper, the tables set with white linen and adorned each with a glowing light in a small plastic pagoda. After the stresses of the day reaction had set in, and he felt too exhausted even for the merry exchange of repartee with Seff.

Seff, on the other hand, looked as fresh as if she had just stepped out of the shower after a blameless night's sleep. "Come on, David," she persisted. "The rising young executive and the last of the old aristocrats? It doesn't add up."

David shrugged. "You were there," he pointed out. "You know as well as I do that but for Gawaine I could be serving time for murder."

Seff took a sip of jasmine tea. "But that's not all. You're not the sort of man who would hang out with someone out of gratitude, and Gawaine is the last person to want you to. And yet here you are."

David considered taking offence at her probing, but he was far too tired. Ordinarily he didn't care to remember the time when he had come within a whisker of being arrested for murder. Without Gawaine's intervention, he would have been, and quite probably tried, convicted and banged up for a good long stretch. As far as he knew, that had been Gawaine's first encounter with murder, too, and he guessed that his friend was even more reluctant to remember those few days, which had been nasty and brutish, but mercifully short.

None of which, David reflected, answered Seff's question, even if he had been prepared to satisfy her curiosity. He only knew that the person he was in Gawaine's company was not quite the same as the one who got up, showered, went to the office every day and probably spent the evening in a wine bar. David found it hard to admit, but he liked that person better than the everyday one. He managed not to analyse what that might mean.

"Yes, here I am," he replied to Seff, who had been steadily working her way through chicken chow mein while he cogitated. "And this is where I'm staying, if it's all the same to you. Without going into detail. This is a restaurant, not a psychiatrist's couch."

To his relief, all Seff did was shrug. "Suit yourself."

Chapter Nineteen

'Eye well things past and present, and let conjectural sagacity suffise for things to come.'
Christian Morals, III.xiii

The inquest on Templeman proceeded as planned. The jury returned a verdict of murder by person or persons unknown. By then Seff's paper was on the streets with an updated account of Gawaine's involvement, and in the Stop Press the account of the attack on him. Seff, not unnaturally, was smug. At the end of the inquest she cut David neatly out of a crowd of her unsuccessful rivals and bore him off.

"I've given Carter those notes," she told him. "Now you can buy me lunch."

"I bought you dinner last night," David protested. "You think you're liberated, you buy me lunch."

Seff gave him a mocking smile. "Anyone would think you weren't grateful for a bed for the night."

And that, David reflected, was not as satisfactory as it sounded. It was not her own bed Seff referred to, but she had, after one in the morning, managed to get him a room in her own hotel. She herself was on the floor above. The thought of climbing the stairs had never crossed David's mind – or at least, had only tiptoed in and out again. He had been far too exhausted; only naked will-power had got him out of bed in time to attend the inquest.

They had lunch in the garden of the Turf, along with about five million American tourists. In the midst of the babble it was easy enough to hold a private conversation.

"What do you do now?" Seff asked.

"I don't know. Gawaine wants me out of Oxford, but I'll stay till Sunday night. I have to be back in London Monday morning, if I want to keep my job."

Seff considered. "How safe is Gawaine in that hospital?"

"Good enough. I checked with Carter, first thing. He has a man on duty."

"And when he comes out?"

That was not as easy to answer. David had assumed, and said so, that it would all be over by the time Gawaine was well enough to leave.

"I doubt it," was Seff's comment. "I think Inspector Carter is worried. He was really grateful for those notes."

"But if Heatherington's prints are on them – "

"What will that prove?" Seff snapped at him. "Just that he's a nosy old so-and-so, and we all knew that already. It doesn't tie him to the attack. To do that, you would need to find his fingerprints or his DNA on the knife, and I'll bet you anything you like they aren't there."

"And he has an alibi for Templeman's murder," David said, dissatisfied.

"Has he? Hang on." Seff whipped out her notebook and scribbled in it, ignoring David's protest. "It's a fake, of course. He did it."

David would have enjoyed his lunch more if he could have been sure of that. He would have enjoyed it more still if he had not felt that every chance remark would turn up in the next day's edition.

"What we need to find out," Seff went on, "is whether he has an alibi for stabbing Gawaine. Come on, David, finish that beer. We've got to get back to St Clement's."

"We?" David inquired.

Seff stared at him. "You're not giving up, are you?"

"Giving up? I hardly even started."

David's comment was muttered, half to himself, and the only response it drew was an exasperated sigh from Seff. He did as he was told and finished his beer, but at the same time he made up his mind that he was going to mutiny if she expected him to play Dr Watson to her Holmes. Gawaine was one thing…

"I'm going to see Gawaine," he announced.

Seff looked less exasperated. "I suppose you are," she agreed, and shrugged amiably. "Okay. I'll go alibi-spotting on my own."

"Try the Chaplain," David suggested, more willing to co-operate if he wasn't expected to involve himself directly. "He must have been around. The service hadn't been over long. And the Dean. I met him myself, just at the other end of the cloisters."

He watched the play of expression on Seff's face as she considered the possibilities. She ended by shaking her head.

"Father Gerard is a pussy-cat," she murmured. "But the Dean, now…" She looked across the table at David, her eyes large and candid. "You do realise, David, that you're giving me a list of suspects for the two murders?"

"Yes, I realise that."

Seff grinned swiftly. "Just as long as you know… Any more?"

"Two more. The Bursar, Colonel Morrison. And – "

"I've met him," Seff interrupted. "He doesn't look old enough to have been getting girls pregnant thirty years ago."

"He was an undergraduate here," David told her.

She scribbled something else. David thought about letting her in on Sue's letter and the reference to 'a soldier' that seemed to point to Morrison, but decided against it. Seff was quite dangerous enough as it was; in any case, it was Heatherington's fingerprint on the letter, not Morrison's.

Seff finished scribbling. "Okay, who's the other?"

"A guy called Porteus. Classics don."

He wondered if he ought to feel guilty about sicking Seff onto Porteus. Probably not. In fact, remembering what the Dean had told him on the previous evening about Gawaine's breakdown – information which later events had pushed out of his mind – definitely not. Porteus could take what was coming to him. And if what was coming to him was Seff's individual brand of harassment, it might even do him good. David felt the warm glow of a job well done as he got up from the table.

"See you later," Seff promised. "Give my love to Gawaine."

"Seff sends her love," David announced.

He was covering considerable shock. He had arrived at the hospital in a comfortably optimistic mood, expecting Gawaine to look better, whereas, if anything, he looked worse. He was haggard, exhausted, and while nothing could entirely subdue him, it was obviously taking a great deal of effort even to talk.

"That was kind," he murmured in reply to David. "How was the inquest?"

"Murder by person or persons unknown," David said, dropping into the chair by the bed. "As we expected. Nothing new. Is there anything you want me to do?"

Gawaine shook his head, a barely perceptible movement.

"You still don't remember anything?" David asked.

This time the shake of the head was more definite. "No. I can't even remember what the idea was I had, but I know it was important. And I'm too wretchedly tired even to think… I can't – "

"You don't have to," David interrupted, and to get his mind off that train of thought, added, "Let me tell you what Seff found."

He launched into the story of the notes in the bin, and was gratified to see Gawaine looking faintly interested. He nodded in agreement when David told him Seff's suspicions of Heatherington.

"Quite likely, my dear David, but why?"

David suddenly felt better. They were discussing the problem again; things were almost back to normal. "You were getting too close," he replied.

Gawaine's expression showed a faint trace of his habitual self-ridicule. "Then he has an unpleasant way of expressing his faith in me. All the same," he went on, "if it was Heatherington, why? He has an alibi for Templeman's murder."

David could only repeat what he had thought of that alibi from the beginning: there must be some way of breaking it.

"And he saw Seff's notes," he concluded. "He knows, or thinks he knows, that you can identify him as the father of Sue's baby."

"If his prints are there," Gawaine reminded him.

"Yes. I'll check on that with Carter. And his alibi. If he has another one, I might run amok with a knife myself."

Gawaine's eyes widened. "My dear David! How perfectly frightful!" More thoughtfully, he said, "He was in Chapel."

"Oh?"

"Looking very pleased with life." Gawaine's voice faded on the last few words. He was growing tired again; the brief animation was failing. Things were not, of course, back to normal, and would not be for a long time.

"I should go," David said.

"No – not yet. I'm all right. Did you leave college?"

"Yes, I said I would."

A sigh of relief followed the words. Gawaine's eyes closed and fluttered open again. "You're not going back there?"

"No, not unless you want me to. Seff has gone to ask about alibis, so I can – "

"Seff?" Gawaine's eyes had widened again, this time in alarm. "David, she shouldn't – those were her notes..."

David tried to be reassuring. "But she doesn't know anything."

"He may think she does." Obviously Gawaine was not going to be reassured.

"Do you want me to go there and root her out – always supposing she lets me?"

Gawaine hesitated, looking distressed.

Before he could reply, David added, "Come on, let me do my chivalrous bit. You know you would go, if you were on your feet."

"All right." Gawaine reached out as David got up and made for the door. "David – for goodness' sake, be careful."

As he negotiated Oxford's one-way system, evidently designed by the tortuous minds of dons to weed out those undergraduates not intelligent enough to find their prospective college, David wondered how serious Gawaine's worries were. Unless the murderer had completely flipped his lid, it was unlikely that he would be skewering indiscriminately. Each further act of violence would make it more likely for him to be caught. Except, of course, that he was now responsible for three, and he had not been caught yet. It was time he was.

Ignoring the porter – not Heatherington – David strode through the lodge and headed resolutely for the Dean's study. Two minutes later he was totally lost. He wasted some time wandering down panelled passages and in and out of doors that seemed to lead to different parts of the garden. Eventually he asked someone whom he presumed to be a passing gardener – he was actually a passing Professor of Philosophy – and found himself knocking at Verner's door.

The familiar grunt invited him in. Opening the door, Gawaine saw that the Dean was not alone. The Master, Edwin Galbraith, was with him, as imposing and acid-faced as ever.

David, unaware of any need to propitiate his eminence, nodded to him and addressed the Dean. "Excuse me, Dr Verner. I wondered if you'd seen Ms Brown."

"Brown? Reporter?" the Dean was beginning, when the Master cut in smoothly.

"I spoke to Miss Brown half an hour or so ago. I'm afraid I had to make it clear to her that her questions were not welcome. I asked her to leave."

David began to visualise how that must have gone down with Seff, but he had to concentrate on the Master, who had drawn breath and was sweeping on.

"I also regret that I feel obliged to take the decision to terminate the private investigation in College. After the publicity I made it quite clear I wished to avoid, not to mention the unfortunate incident involving Mr St Clair..."

He continued to pontificate, though David, well aware that the 'unfortunate incident' had come within a whisker of being a third murder, was too indignant to pay much attention. He also suspected that Galbraith, far from being concerned about Gawaine, was simply using the attack as an excuse to get rid of someone he had never wanted there in the first place. He heard Verner growling under his breath, something that might have been a much ruder equivalent of the word 'rubbish'. For once David agreed with him.

"...and obviate the risk of further such unfortunate incidents," the Master finished.

"You're asking me to leave?" David queried, to be sure he had it straight.

"I fear so."

"Right. With pleasure." He took out the key Verner

had lent him the night before and planked it down on the desk at his elbow. “Your key, Dr Verner.”

The Dean twitched an eyebrow at it. “Seen St Clair?” he asked. “How was he?”

“Not good.”

“I’m sorry.”

“So am I.”

David wished them both a good afternoon and walked out. There had been a certain amount of satisfaction in that. He wondered as he left the college again – he hoped for the last time – whether Seff had found out anything before they bounced her. And, having been bounced, where did she go? Certainly she would not have stopped asking questions. Unable to think of anything better, David got into his car and set off for the hotel.

Chapter Twenty

'...irregular apprehensions of things, perverted notions, conceptions, and incurable hallucinations.'

The Garden of Cyrus, IV

As he drove back to the hotel, David felt worried. There was a first time for everything, even for being worried about Seff Brown. Of course she could take care of herself – far more efficiently than Gawaine – but the fact remained that she had been last seen in St Clement's College, where nasty things happened to people who asked too many questions.

David wondered where else she might be, if he failed to find her at the hotel. Not with the other reporters; she got too much fun out of running rings round them. He thought about going back to the hospital to consult Gawaine, but that was obviously impossible. Gawaine might be already fretting himself into a state when David had not reported that he had found Seff. Telling him she had disappeared would be asking for trouble. David regretted that he had never asked Seff for her mobile number.

After all that, she had not disappeared. David overtook her a couple of hundred yards from the hotel, swinging along as if she hadn't a care in the world. With a smart toot on his horn he drew into the side of the road and opened his door.

"Kerb-crawling now?" she asked as she slid into the passenger seat.

David ignored that as all part of the merry give-and-take of conversation with Seff. "I hear you got bounced?" he said.

"Right." Seff gave him a swift, sideways grin. "But not before I found out most of what I wanted to know. "No – " she directed as David began signalling to turn into the hotel car park. "I'm not stopping here. I was on my way to the Morrisons."

There were various possible responses to that, of which David considered, "Walk," or "Take your own car." However, he made none of them, simply continuing to drive.

"You went there with Gawaine," Seff said, more statement than question.

"Yes."

The pause dragged itself out, David being visited by what was then an unwelcome memory of Gawaine airily demonstrating his total incomprehension of Oxford science – or at least, that was the impression he took pains to give.

Seff finally broke the silence by asking, "Don't you want to know what I found out in College?"

"About..?" David was finding it hard to get his brain back into working order.

"Alibis for stabbing Gawaine, for goodness' sake. Listen. I didn't try to question the Dean, because he was lurking in the cloister, so I assume he could have done it. Father Gerard told me that he spoke to Gawaine at the end of the service, and that Gawaine stayed in the chapel, he thought to meditate. Father Gerard went back to the vestry, put various bits and pieces away, and then went to his rooms. No corroboration."

After her first few words, David started to get involved in spite of himself. Leaving a minimum of attention for the road, he commented, "He could have done it. He knew Gawaine was there."

"Yes, true, but I don't believe it. I told you, he's a pussy-cat. Heatherington is far more likely. He says that he went to the service, but left straight afterwards and went to his pub for a drink. Inspector Carter will have to check that one."

"And the others?"

"I didn't manage to see Colonel Morrison. That's why I want to go to his house now. With any luck, the Master won't have bothered to ring up and tell him I was bounced."

David drove on, overtook a bus with what he felt was a certain amount of panache, and considered the name Seff had not mentioned. "What about Porteus?"

Seff said nothing for a minute. She obviously had a choice bit of news and was enjoying tantalising him with it. At last she said, "Rock solid alibi."

"Not another one!"

"Apparently he was addressing some sort of dining club, on the other side of Oxford. He was there for pre-dinner drinks at about the time the Chapel service started, ate his meal and read his paper in full view of about thirty assorted members of the university, and came home, wined and dined and totally ignorant, while we were at the hospital. I haven't been able to check it, but the police will, and he couldn't lie about something as obvious as that."

David thought about it. Certainly it seemed impossible to suborn thirty respected pillars of the community to substantiate a non-existent alibi.

"He didn't slip out at all?"

"He says not. It would have taken too long. And in any case, why? He didn't know Gawaine would be alone in Chapel."

David had to admit the logic of that, but there was still something about Seff's story that puzzled him. "Porteus told you all that?"

"Yes."

"Willingly?"

"Why not?"

There was no obvious reason why not, except that Porteus, confronted by Gawaine, had made it quite clear, in unpleasant and unequivocal terms, that he would speak to no-one but the police. Why, David asked Seff, should he make an exception in her case?

"Perhaps I fluttered my eyelashes at him."

David made the sound that is spelt 'Hah!' He had yet to see the day when Seff would flutter her eyelashes at anyone, and he would not have picked on Porteus as a man likely to be susceptible if she did. It was odd, he thought, and Gawaine had taught him to look out for things that were odd, that Porteus had given his alibi so freely. Unless, of course, that this time he had nothing to hide, when on the previous occasion he was concealing a meeting with Templeman, as proved by his possession of the reprint. Seff, David reminded himself, knew nothing of the reprint.

"Anyway, after that," she continued, apparently seeing nothing worth discussing in Porteus' behaviour, "I went to see Inspector Carter. He's had the notes fingerprinted." Again her eyes were dancing as she paused, but this time David could guess what she had to tell. "They were Heatherington's prints. I was right!"

"Well done."

For once there was no sarcasm in his praise; no-one else, with the possible exception of Gawaine, would have seen any significance in the notes still remaining in the bin.

"There were no prints on the knife, though," Seff went on. "Just an ordinary college kitchen knife. Anyone could have got hold of it, though it might have been easier for Heatherington than anyone else. David, I'm sure he did it! But they won't be able to tag him with it, unless they can break his alibi for Monday morning."

She pulled down the car's vanity mirror and peered at herself. "Once I've spoken to the Bursar," she said, "I'll have to ease off. As far as investigating goes, I'm out of it." She folded back the mirror, apparently well-satisfied with the results of her scrutiny.

"So are you and Gawaine," she added. "It's probably just as well. If this gets solved, it will be the police who do it. And I've got a funny feeling that they aren't going to get any more information. If he sits tight, he stands a good chance of getting away with it."

David was thinking over this assessment of their chances – as uncompromisingly realistic as anything Seff had said – as he drew up outside the Morrisons' house.

"Very nice," Seff commented as she got out of the car. "Nice house, nice road. He wouldn't want to lose it, would he?"

If that was meant to convey that she suspected Morrison, David could not work out why. He had told her nothing of Sue's letter. He was still thinking about it as she rang the doorbell, and suddenly began to wonder – in the midst of the usual outbreak of barking – what excuse they had for being there. There was, of course, the invitation to dinner on the following evening, though he could easily have phoned to cancel that.

Colonel Morrison opened the door as David decided that would have to be his line. This time he was dressed more casually in jeans and a polo shirt, and looked much more comfortable, in David's eyes, than in his formal College wear.

Seff took the initiative, introducing herself and asking the Bursar if he had any comments on the situation. It quickly became clear to David that here, if anywhere, Seff had met her match.

"Oh, yes, yes." Morrison interrupted her questions with good-humoured impatience. "Terrible business. And you can quote me, young woman, if it does you any good. Come in and have some tea."

He led them down the passage to the kitchen, which on this occasion seemed to be full of children and dog, along with a golden, haughty-looking cat, which clearly had no doubts about who was in control. David felt a pang that Gawaine was not with them. He would have liked the cat.

Morrison surveyed them all with fatherly affection. "I sneaked out of college," he admitted, "to start the weekend early. Thank God it's Friday, that's what I always say."

Mrs Morrison, realising she had visitors, turned away

from the cooker as they entered. "Come in," she said. "Sit down if you can find somewhere. I'll make some fresh tea."

David could see that family tea was just coming to an end. The children were in the process of polishing off everything in sight, and arguing amiably about which TV programme to watch. The cocker spaniel sat at their feet, in the hope of something edible being dropped, by accident or design. David made himself a space and sat, while Seff perched on a kitchen stool and hopefully took out her notebook.

"I'm glad you came round," Mrs Morrison went on to David. "I wanted to tell you how shocked we were to hear about Gawaine. How is he?"

"He'll be all right," David replied, not wanting to go into detail. "I thought I ought to say, about tomorrow night…"

"I know, I'm sorry. I was looking forward to it. Of course you're very welcome to come, but I don't suppose you're in the mood?"

David agreed that he was not in the mood, while Seff tapped her pen restively, and as soon as she could get a word in, asked the Colonel, "You weren't in college yourself yesterday evening?"

Morrison stared at her, seemed to consider taking offence, and then laughed. "You want my alibi, I suppose? Well, I wasn't in college. I was back here when Evensong started, with my feet up, drinking a glass of sherry. Isn't that right?" he appealed to his wife.

Mrs Morrison nodded as she put cups of tea down beside Seff and David. One of the children, after an eloquent prod, came round and offered a biscuit barrel.

"You didn't dine in college, then?" Seff asked.

"No." The Colonel grimaced. "To tell you the truth, I hardly ever do, if I can help it. Too much food, too much drink, too much nonsense being talked. And don't quote me on that, if you don't mind."

"Yet you dined in college that Sunday evening – the time you had the stomach upset." Seff blinked innocently at the Colonel. "Didn't that disturb your week-end, going into college on a Sunday?"

David felt a reluctant twinge of admiration for Seff. It was odd that the Bursar had been in college then. He hadn't considered that, and as far as he knew, neither had Gawaine.

It was Mrs Morrison who replied. "I'd taken the children to see their grandparents. Michael couldn't go because he had a set of accounts to work on."

Colonel Morrison nodded. If he was surprised that she should revert to his alibi for Monday, he did not show it. He watched Seff for a minute as she scribbled, and remarked, "You're sure you're from a newspaper, and not the cops?"

"Have they been here?" David asked, thinking it might be as well not to follow up that question.

"Not here," Morrison replied. "A sergeant had a word with me in college, earlier today. I couldn't tell him anything."

Unfortunately, he wasn't telling anything now, either, though David had to admit that might be because he had nothing to tell. Once again he wished Gawaine had been there, because he might have known the right questions to ask, but David himself had no idea where to go now.

He was slightly reassured to find that Seff had no idea, either, and was putting her notebook away. There was nothing more to do. The Bursar had an alibi for both occasions – admittedly one that depended on his wife – and the man exuded innocence. Somehow he did not seem to fit into the St Clement's mould. All the other suspects, in their way, were eccentric; Morrison, on the other hand – affectionate husband and father, soldier and dog-lover – was extraordinarily normal. Surely there was no twist in him that might have led to murder?

Seff began to take her leave, and David followed suit, taking with him good wishes for Gawaine and promises to renew the invitation at the earliest possible opportunity. One of the children, no doubt on politeness fatigues, was detailed to escort them off the premises. It – the track suit and mop of hair gave David no clue as to gender – did so with a rather awed look that suggested it was thoroughly relishing its proximity to murder.

He never knew what to say to children, and was going out of the garden gate with no more than a goodbye, but Seff, as she turned to leave, inquired brightly, "Are you glad your Daddy's better?"

The child's awed look gave way to one that was probably more familiar: the recognition that an adult was being predictably thick.

"Daddy hasn't been ill," it said.

Chapter Twenty-One

'...swarms and millions of Rhapsodies, begotten only to distract and abuse the weaker judgements of Scholars, and to maintain the trade and mystery of Typographers.'
Religio Medici

David grabbed Seff, who seemed disposed to linger, and hustled her into the car. She was sparkling.

"Well!" she exclaimed. "What about that?"

"What about it?" David asked; he did not really need an exposition from Seff, but it was as well to keep an unpleasant truth at arm's length for as long as possible.

"Daddy hasn't been ill," Seff repeated. "Except that according to the official version, Daddy was kept up half Sunday night, and not fit to go into work on Monday."

"The kid might not have known," David protested half-heartedly.

"Kids know everything," Seff declared in a tone that permitted no contradiction. "And if you'd let me carry on," she added irritably, "I might have found out what Daddy was doing."

David could see that the Morrison moppet was still there, swinging on the gate and staring at the car with undisguised fascination. Before Seff could make a bid for freedom, he switched on the ignition and drew away.

"I'll take you back to the hotel," he said.

Seff sighed. "You're a moral coward, David."

"I just don't like the thought of interrogating kids."

The sigh was repeated, definitely annoyed now. "Who's talking about interrogating? I wasn't going to put it up against a wall with a rubber hosepipe, you know. I have got experience in talking to kids. I know how to deal with them."

"Then you shouldn't be asking one to shop its Dad."

David had thought at first that Seff's question to the child had just been for the sake of conversation, but he was rapidly coming to realise that it had been very carefully calculated to get the information she wanted in return. In fact, he would not have been surprised if Seff's primary reason for visiting the Morrisons at all had been for the chance of having a word with one of the children.

"Come on, David," she was protesting now. "Don't be so stuffy. We've cracked it, for Heaven's sake! His Monday alibi is a load of old rope. And that means his alibi for last night is no good, either. Mrs M has been lying in her teeth."

Irrelevantly David remembered Gawaine's half-serious designation of the murderer as M. Had he been more accurate than he knew? There was Sue's letter, too, with its reference to a soldier. Things suddenly looked very bad for Colonel Morrison.

"Don't you want to get there before Gawaine for once?" Seff asked.

"If Gawaine couldn't get there without questioning a child about its father, he wouldn't get there at all."

David knew he sounded stuffy, exactly as Seff had accused him, but it had to be said.

Seff cast her eyes up to heaven – or to the portion of car roof that was in the way. "Gawaine has a right to his scruples," she said incisively. "You don't."

David ignored the reflection on his moral standards. He was suddenly conscious of nothing but an overwhelming desire to talk this new development over with Gawaine. And at the same time he realised how impossible that was. He could not see what to do. It was unthinkable to go and see Gawaine and tell him nothing, but if he told him about this new development Gawaine would be deeply upset and worried, and he was in no fit state to cope. If he could keep it quiet for a day or two…

David went on driving in silence, thinking it over, while Seff, her expression as smug as the Morrisons' cat, took out her notebook and began to scribble again.

They said nothing more until David had put the car in the hotel car park.

"Thanks for the lift, David," Seff said. "I want to go in and freshen up, and then we'll go and see Inspector Carter."

"We'll do what?"

Seff paid no attention to the question. She was already on her way into the hotel.

David caught her up at the reception desk, asking for her messages. "Listen, I'm not – "

The receptionist handed Seff a note.

"Shut up, David." Seff scanned the note quickly. "It's my editor. He wants me to ring him. Go upstairs, David, and I'll give you a call when I've finished." Pulling out her mobile, she withdrew into the hotel lounge, deserted at this hour of the day, without waiting for a response.

Unwilling to be ordered around, and particularly

by Seff Brown – Gawaine managed the same thing with altogether more charm – David still withdrew to his room. He had half a mind to sneak out again, and simply not be available, but in the end he stayed, if only because he wanted to know exactly what move Seff would make next.

He had not waited long when he heard hurried footsteps coming up the stairs, past the door to his room, and on up the next flight. Seff. David felt a definite twinge of annoyance that she hadn't come in, after giving him his instructions so clearly, and considered all over again the possibility of leaving her to stew, before following her to her room.

There was no reply when he knocked. From inside the room he could hear miscellaneous thumpings and bangings, and he half wondered whether there was a fight going on inside. Someone had been lying in wait for her... Then he realised how absurd that was, knocked again, and pushed the door open.

The bangings were being made by Seff herself, opening and closing drawers and cupboards and hurling her assorted possessions in the general direction of a holdall on the bed. She was quite clearly in a flaming temper. When she caught sight of David she had a hairdryer in her hand, and there was a nasty couple of seconds when he thought it might connect with his head.

"Hi," he said.

Seff smouldered at him. "What do you want?"

"I thought I'd been commanded to make myself available."

Seff made an inarticulate sound of contempt and began stuffing things into the holdall. She was ignoring David.

"Are you leaving?" he asked.

"No, I'm doing this for the exercise."

David tried again. "Why are you leaving?"

This time Seff condescended to stop packing and acknowledge his existence. "I've been pulled off the story, that's why."

"Pulled off? You're not serious?"

"Oh yes, I am." Suddenly Seff went off the boil and sat down on the side of the bed, pulling a scarf through her fingers and looking unusually miserable. "You heard me say there was a message to phone my editor. He pulled me off. Told me to come back to the office. Just as if I'd made a mess of it."

"But you haven't," David protested. "That was a great story this morning. A scoop."

Seff gave him a lopsided smile. "True. But that was this morning."

"So what happened?"

Seff started the packing again, more neatly this time, and told him, "My editor didn't say, not in so many words, but he said enough, so I could read between the lines. He's had a directive from on high. Our Proprietor didn't like the way I was handling it."

"I still don't get it."

Seff straightened up and faced him. "When I was in college – oh, come in, David, for crying out loud, and shut the door. I'm not going to bite you. Sit down somewhere out of my way."

David chose, cautiously, an upright chair that he judged was well out of the firing line.

"When I was in college," Seff went on, "the Master told

me that he didn't want me around. And I'll bet the first thing he did after I left was to phone Our Proprietor and get me called back in."

"Could he do that?"

Seff shrugged. "How else? These people, they were all at school together, or university, or they go to the same garden parties. Galbraith thought I was a nuisance, he made that quite clear. And I made it quite clear that I intended going on being a nuisance, with or without his permission. And so..."

She shrugged again and went back to her packing. David watched in silence. It had not occurred to him earlier, but now he was wondering whether there was any significance in the Master's having decided to close the investigation, and on top of that, to use his influence to get rid of an inconveniently nosy journalist. Had anyone bothered to look at Galbraith's alibis? But then, he remembered, Galbraith had not been at St Clement's when Sue's murder had taken place. Trying to connect him was probably a waste of mental effort. And besides, they had just managed to pin it on Morrison.

It was not until she was zipping up the bag that Seff spoke again. "Aren't you going to ask me what I'm going to do now?"

"I was afraid I might get that flight bag round the ears."

For reply, Seff lifted the bag and hefted it in one hand, her eyes narrowed. Then she dropped it back on the bed and sat down again, smiling reluctantly.

"You might have, at that. Listen, David, I've got to go back to London, if I expect to have a job waiting for me, but that's no reason why we can't go and see Inspector Carter first."

"I don't want to see Carter."

Seff's smile vanished, and her somewhat softened mood with it. "Why not?"

There was no real, logical reason why not. All David could say was, "I'm worried about Gawaine."

For some reason that did not provoke the shower of freezing contempt that he had expected. Seff nodded seriously. "I know. I know he won't like it. But you can't really suggest that we should suppress evidence because Gawaine might be upset." She paused and added, "He wouldn't do it, would he?"

David was silent. Seff was not to know that Gawaine was already suppressing evidence, about Porteus and the reprint, though perhaps that was irrelevant now. And she was right that he would never shield a murderer, knowing him to be a murderer, whatever his personal feelings might be. But this wasn't quite the same…

"I'd like to talk it over first," he said.

"But I haven't time. Look, David, this is my job. I've got to be in the thick of things. I've found something out, I've got to report it to Carter, and – "

"That's it, isn't it?" David interrupted. "All you care about is your bloody scandal sheet."

Seff's voice was soft with fury. "My paper is not a scandal sheet, and it's very far from all I care about, as you would know if you weren't so mind-bogglingly stupid. This is new evidence about Templeman's murder – "

David interrupted again. "Are you going to tell Carter how you got it?"

"Oh, here we go again! One question, that was all. I'm not ashamed of it. I'm going, and I want you to come because you're a witness."

In spite of being angry with her, for a moment David nearly gave in. It was true, they had evidence that proved Morrison's alibi was worthless. The police had to know.

"For goodness' sake," Seff snapped, "he's killed two people, and very nearly killed a third."

Somehow that decided David – to do the opposite of what she hoped. He did not want to take the responsibility.

"No," he said.

"No? What do you mean, no?"

"I mean no. It's too serious. I can't stop you going to Carter, but I'm going to talk it over with Gawaine."

Seff's lips tightened, and David braced himself, but her voice when she spoke was perfectly level. "All right, David, but I'll have to tell Carter you were there. You can expect to be questioned."

David shrugged. There was nothing to say.

Seff picked up her bag and made for the door, but before she reached it, she hesitated. "Tell Gawaine I'm sorry."

She left without arguing any more.

David saw her off, restraining himself with no great difficulty from offering to carry her bag down, and waiting while she checked out. For several minutes he stood watching the spot where her black Mini had disappeared. He knew she was doing the right thing as she saw it. In a way, he knew himself that it was right. But he still wished he had been able to persuade her to let Gawaine know first.

Feeling irritable without really knowing why, David went back to his own car. He had better get to the hospital and bring Gawaine up to date before he heard it from anyone else. Seff had not left him the option of keeping it quiet. Stupid, perhaps, to have thought that she would. And stupid, after all, to feel despondent when the case was eventually at an end. He hardly put into words, even to himself, his faint hope that Gawaine might still be able to see a loophole.

Chapter Twenty-Two

'I have shaken hands with delight.'
Religio Medici

"I don't know if you can see a loophole, but I certainly can't."

In Gawaine's room at the hospital, David was finishing a careful account of what Seff had found out, including her questioning of the Morrison child. Gawaine had listened intently, not interrupting, eyes fixed on David's face. As David stopped speaking, he let out a sigh and shook his head in discouragement.

"I shouldn't be bothering you with it..." David said.

Gawaine raised a hand, gently silencing him. "I need to know," he murmured. "If there's any sense in this... I wish I could talk to Morrison. Do you think he would come here?"

David jerked his head in the direction of the door. "There's a cop out there," he said. "With strict instructions to let no-one in who might possibly – "

"But I can't believe that Morrison..."

David overrode him. "He lied about where he was. So did his wife."

He was starting to sound aggressive, and Gawaine's faint smile informed him of it. "That isn't proof," he pointed out.

"It may not be proof, but as far as I'm concerned, it's good enough to be going on with. No-one in this case is coming anywhere near you."

Gawaine tried a shrug, caught the movement with a slight intake of breath, and fluttered a hand in protest. "If I had any information, surely I've passed it on by now? He couldn't possibly think I'm still worth killing?"

"If you assume he's rational, no," David replied sombrely. "I'm not convinced of that."

Gawaine held his gaze for a moment and then nodded in acquiescence. "You could have a point." His voice was fading as weariness took over. "But still, I can't see Morrison… It has the wrong feel to it, somehow."

"If you ask me, there's a hell of a lot in this business that has the wrong feel."

It was time to go. David got to his feet, wishing there was more that he could do, that Gawaine did not look so frail, and more than anything that the whole affair could be over and done with. He wanted to say something encouraging, but could think of nothing better than, "Don't worry. Inspector Carter will know how to handle it."

If so, the Inspector was taking it very quietly. David was summoned to his office to make a statement, about what the Morrison child had said, but apart from warning him not to visit the Bursar's family again, Carter gave him no information. No arrest had been made by the time David left Oxford the next morning.

In the following week, David caught up with work and managed to convince his boss that his time away had been spent productively. He didn't have much leisure, or mental energy, to think about the murders at St Clement's.

On the Friday evening, he had barely entered his flat, shrugged out of his jacket and started to wonder what to do about dinner, when his phone rang. Gawaine's voice came down the line, sounding faint and shaky.

"David…are you busy this evening?"

"Gawaine!" For the moment David ignored the question. "What's going on? Are you still in hospital?"

"No, I discharged myself. I'm still in Oxford, though. I – "

"Are you completely out of your mind?" David interrupted. "You're not in St Clement's are you?"

There was a kind of tired humour in Gawaine's reply. "No, I haven't quite got a death wish. I'm in the hotel where you and Seff stayed."

"And you want me there?"

"If you can bear it." Now Gawaine sounded uncertain. "I know how much you hated it… Only, you see – " His voice tightened. "I know who killed them."

David knew he was gaping. "You know?"

"Yes," Gawaine said nervily. "It all fits. Why he killed Sue – and why he didn't report it as an accident – and how Templeman came to have the letter – and what Sue meant by 'a soldier like his Dad'. It's really quite straight-forward."

"So who – " David was beginning, but Gawaine interrupted him, probably not even aware that he had spoken.

"Now I've got to finish what I started. And I…"

"You want me there?"

One word, penitent and ashamed. "Yes."

"Book a room for me. Then stay in your room and lock the door. I'm on my way."

The long summer evening was drawing to a close and the street lights were coming on by the time David pulled off the road and found a space in the hotel car park. He was checking in when Gawaine appeared at the foot of the stairs. He stood silently to one side until David had received his room key.

David was shocked at the sight of him. He was used to Gawaine's fragile appearance, and his ability to seem, at very short notice, in imminent danger of complete collapse, but now he looked haggard, as if physical pain and mental stress had brought him close to the end of his endurance. He made no protest when David took him by the elbow and hustled him back upstairs to David's own room. David deposited his overnight bag on the bed and Gawaine in the one armchair, then stood over him.

"Well?"

Gawaine raised a hand to his head. "I'm frightfully sorry..."

"You know you shouldn't be here at all," David went on, battling with unreasonable fury. "Why on earth did they let you out?"

"I talked them into it." Gawaine let out a weary sigh. "I'll be perfectly all right, David, once I get this business sorted out."

"Why you?" David demanded. "Why not just phone Carter and dump the whole problem in his lap?"

"If only... No, there's one more piece of evidence I need to find, and for that I have to go back to St Clement's."

David let out a snort. "Bad idea. You'll only tangle with the Master's Rottweiler."

A gleam of humour woke in Gawaine's eyes. "Yes, or his battle-trained tarantulas. The fact remains, I can't proceed without this one last item, and I have to go to St Clement's to get it."

He started to stand up, and David put out a hand to stop him. "Oh, no. You're going nowhere tonight. It's far too late."

Gawaine made a small sound of protest, but sank back into the chair without trying to argue.

"Have you eaten?" David asked. "No? Right, then I'm going to phone room service, and you're going to tell me what's been happening, and what this one vital item is." When he had rung down for sandwiches and coffee, he continued. "So. Tell me how you managed to nail Morrison."

Gawaine looked up, infinitesimally more alert. "I haven't. Nor will I."

"But why not?" David stared at his friend in astonishment. "He hasn't an alibi. And he must be Sue's soldier..."

Gawaine shook his head. He had obviously been thinking things over since David reported to him in hospital, and he sounded much more sure of himself.

"My dear David, that's not logical. What Seff proved was that Colonel Morrison did not have a stomach upset – which we strongly suspected all along. It does not logically follow that he was in college murdering Templeman. We pointed out from the very beginning that Mrs Morrison made her phone call before Sue's body was discovered.

The inference is surely that Morrison had urgent business elsewhere."

David thought that over as he went to sit opposite Gawaine in the window-seat. "You mean he was up to something he didn't want the College to know about?"

"Precisely."

"And do you know what?"

"Inspector Carter has been questioning the Colonel. Extensively. I understand that he certainly would have been arrested, but for the anomaly of Heatherington's fingerprint on the letter. However, Morrison admitted that he hadn't been ill, but he insisted he hadn't been in college. He also refused to say where he had been."

"Then he was up to no good!" David exclaimed. "Another woman – "

"Really, my dear David!" Gawaine interrupted. "Another woman – and he asked his wife to give him an alibi? It would show a certain style, I admit, but...what does go on in the circles you move in? No, as it happens, there was nothing immoral, or criminal, in what he was doing."

"Then where was he?"

Gawaine sighed, and passed a hand across his eyes. He was obviously finding it difficult to co-ordinate his ideas. David knew that he really should not be questioning him.

"I stopped off to see Mrs Morrison on my way here, after I left hospital. I intended trying to convince her that her husband should tell the police the truth. As it happened, that wasn't necessary. He'd gone to do exactly that."

David frowned, puzzled. "Why? After all this time..."

"Because the situation has changed. Once you know what Morrison was doing that Monday morning, his actions become quite reasonable."

"So what was he doing?" David demanded impatiently.

"He was at a job interview."

David was stunned to silence. Gawaine, though obviously tired, managed a faint smile. "Apparently, although Morrison took on the post of Bursar when he came out of the army, he never intended to stay there permanently. But he felt that it would be better for himself and the College if he said nothing until he had a definite position fixed up. On the Monday when Templeman was murdered, he was in London, having an interview at a merchant bank, and three very high-powered people are prepared to back him up."

"So why didn't he say so from the beginning?"

"He didn't want to mess up his chances of the job," Gawaine replied. "However, this morning he had a definite offer – "

"Good for him."

" – so Mrs Morrison was quite ready to tell me all about it, while he went down to see Carter. They hadn't enjoyed lying in the first place, but once they started, they didn't have much choice about going on. I think they were both relieved to be making a clean breast of it. He didn't kill anyone, David."

David, needing to think that over, was quite glad that his bell rang at that moment with his room service order. When he came back to put the tray on the table, he saw that Gawaine seemed to have relaxed a little, lying back in his chair with eyes closed.

"So Morrison is clean as a whistle," David remarked as he put Gawaine's coffee and sandwich down on the occasional table beside his chair.

Gawaine nodded.

"Then who is Sue's soldier?"

A faint sigh, but no other response.

"And you haven't been back to St Clement's?"

"Emphatically not. Yet."

David wondered when Gawaine intended telling him the rest. With the Bursar out of the way, the field of suspects was wide open again. He couldn't imagine what it was that had made Gawaine so certain that this time he knew the truth.

For some reason he found himself saying, "The Dean told me about your…your breakdown."

He thought Gawaine stiffened slightly. "Oh yes, that."

"Do you mind? That I know about it?"

"No."

"He thinks you should go back."

Gawaine opened his eyes at that, but somehow it distanced him. "The world of scholarship, my dear David, is scarcely diminished by my loss." After a moment he added, with a faint bitterness that was entirely unlike him, "I've established a reputation for running away. But this time it's a case of *reculer pour mieux sauter*. They won't like it."

He roused himself and picked up his coffee. They ate in silence for a while until Gawaine continued.

"I thought I'd finished with it all," he explained. "I really thought I had. But I woke quite early this morning, and everything seemed so much more…more possible, you see, and I remembered the idea I had that night in Chapel… And then everything fell into place. And that's why I have to go to college in the morning."

"Why?" David asked. "Why can't you let Carter handle it?"

"I told you, there's one more piece of evidence I want to look for. And if I find it, I want to speak to the Dean – before the police. I had a chat with Inspector Carter this afternoon. It will take him a day or two at least to check up on what I told him."

"And what did you tell him?"

Gawaine sipped the last of his coffee, put aside the cup and sank back in the armchair with a gesture that conveyed total nervous prostration. However, when he spoke his voice was quiet but level.

"I told him to have a look at Heatherington's bank account. That was originally your idea."

"The blackmail? You told him to look for payments out of his account?"

Gawaine gave him a blank stare. "Oh, no, my dear David. I told him to look for payments in."

Chapter Twenty-Three

'...a Retrograde cognition of times past, and things which have already been, is more satisfactory than a suspended Knowledge of what is yet unexistent.'

Christian Morals, III.xiii

The astonishing statement about Heatherington's bank account was all David could get out of Gawaine. He did not try very hard. When they first met, he had found his friend's insistence on keeping his knowledge to himself until the very end an irritating affectation, intolerably theatrical. Now he knew it rose from an almost unbearable reluctance to speak at all. Telling the story once took so much out of him, he could not be expected to tell it more than once. So in spite of his own consuming curiosity, David said nothing, let Gawaine depart to his own room without protest, and tried without much success to sleep.

The following morning they headed back into the city centre. In deference to Gawaine's condition, David had moderated his driving, but it was the one occasion when Gawaine, eyes bright and concentrated, but inward-looking, was probably not aware of it.

As they drove down the High Street, Gawaine directed him to drive past St Clement's and across Magdalen Bridge, and find a parking space – not the easiest thing in the world – somewhere up the Cowley Road. They walked back and approached the college from the rear.

"I don't want Heatherington to know we're here. And I don't want to be stopped," Gawaine murmured.

"By the Master?"

"Or the police."

David was not too keen on the sound of that. He thought it over as they entered college by a back gate, crossed a stretch of garden and arrived outside the Dean's door by a completely different route.

"If he's not in, we're in trouble," Gawaine commented.

David thought they were probably in trouble in any case, but he refrained from saying so. Fortunately, as Gawaine knocked, Verner's voice told them to enter. He was sitting at his desk, tapping away on his laptop and wreathed in pipe smoke. When he swivelled round and saw Gawaine, his tangled eyebrows shot up, and it was with a look of disfavour that he said, "I thought you'd gone home."

"As you see, no."

The look of disfavour intensified. "Then what are you doing here?"

"Solving your murders, Dean," Gawaine replied swiftly. "Which was, if you recall, my original remit. However, I shall need your co-operation. Is Dr Porteus available?"

David was trying to catch up with the implications of that; the Dean, however, had other things on his mind.

"Galbraith know you're here?"

"I considered, Dean, that we might bring this to a conclusion without…er…discommoding the Master."

For some reason, what Gawaine said caused the Dean's

gnarled features to break into an evil grin. "Could have a point there," he conceded. "Now, what's all this about Porteus?"

"I want to search his rooms."

Dr Verner gaped. Matters concerning the finance of the late twelfth century were not usually so disconcerting, and could be handled at his leisure.

"Are you telling me – ?"

"I'm telling you nothing at present," Gawaine returned coolly. "I'm making a request. Can you keep Dr Porteus away from his rooms for about half an hour, and give me the key?"

Verner hesitated. David had time to wonder several things: did the Dean really want the murders cleared up; if not, was it because he himself was implicated; would he co-operate because that was the only way to demonstrate his innocence, or would he hide behind authority?

Eventually the Dean took a key from his pocket, unlocked a drawer of his desk, and selected another key, which he held out to Gawaine.

"Only hope you know what you're doing," he grunted. He levered himself up from his chair. "I'll go over there. Give me ten minutes. If you bump into the Master, you're on your own."

"We don't know you, 007," David muttered as the Dean went out.

When the door had closed behind him, David turned to Gawaine. "Do you mean Porteus did it?" The question was really off limits, but he couldn't restrain himself. "He has an alibi for stabbing you," he reminded his friend.

Gawaine nodded abstractedly. He was keyed up now,

poised, waiting; David realised he knew exactly what to do and why. Nervous excitement would carry him through to the end; of course, there would be a reaction afterwards.

Gawaine paced the room until the ten minutes were almost up. Then he stopped, facing David. "You don't have to come."

"Of course I'm coming."

Gawaine went on as if he had not spoken. "I'm not sure if I'm breaking and entering, since Verner gave me the key. But I am sure I'm doing something I shouldn't, and if I'm caught at it, or if I make a cat's breakfast of explaining why, there may be trouble."

"You won't make a cat's breakfast."

Gawaine smiled. "Your faith in me, my dear David, is touching, but it may be misplaced. However, if you insist..." He went to the door, opened it and glanced out. "I believe the appropriate phrase is, 'Let's go.'"

A few minutes later he was inserting the key in the door of Dr Porteus's rooms. They went in. Everything was quiet; Verner had obviously found an excuse to get Porteus away.

"What are we looking for?" David asked.

'Trouble' was the obvious answer; Gawaine did not give it, or any other that satisfied David.

"If you could stay by the door, and listen for Porteus coming back, then I can get on. If anyone knocks, of course, we ignore it. Or the phone."

David did as he was told, and watched Gawaine as he began his search, starting with the desk. Almost at once he pointed out a pamphlet with a striking photograph of the statue of a horse on its cover.

"Templeman's reprint. Still here."

He went through the desk, found nothing, and moved into the bedroom. David passed the time by wondering what it could be that Gawaine was looking for. Something fairly small, if it could be contained in a desk drawer. But David could think of nothing in the case that was missing. The only weapon, other than the force of gravity, was the knife that had stabbed Gawaine, and the police had that. A letter, David thought – the rest of Sue's letter? But then, why were Porteus's fingerprints not on the page they had? And Gawaine did not seem to be looking for a letter; at least, he had ignored the bookshelves, when it would be easy enough to slip a few sheets of paper into the pages of a book.

David thought he might suggest that, when several things happened at once. Standing close to the outer door, he heard the faint sound of footsteps, and almost immediately voices, the bass growls of Verner and Porteus's tenor, apparently lifted in protest. There was another voice, too, that David did not immediately recognise.

David turned towards the bedroom. "Gawaine!"

The footsteps were mounting the staircase; they were cut off. Verner must have thought he had given them long enough, or had just been unable to keep Porteus away from his rooms any longer.

Then Gawaine appeared from the bedroom; his eyes were bright with triumph and he held something small in the palm of his hand.

The door opened. Porteus stepped in, with the Dean, looking helpless, a pace behind. The third man was the Master, Edwin Galbraith. He pushed his way to the front of the group, staring at Gawaine in mingled shock and fury.

My secretary told me she'd seen you, and I couldn't believe it!" he said. "This is an outrage! I warn you, she's calling the police."

"Thank you, Master," Porteus said. "Dean, do you know anything about this?" His voice was rising, high and out of control.

Gawaine, in contrast, was quiet as he said, "I had hoped to discuss this without involving Inspector Carter, at least initially, but if that's your preference, Master, who am I to argue?"

He came forward and held out his hand. David could see the tiny object resting on his palm. It was a wedding ring.

Chapter Twenty-Four

'Men do not easily continue a counterfeiting Life, or dissemble unto Death.'

Christian Morals, III.xx

The meeting had adjourned to the Master's sitting room. Minor matters had delayed them, for example Porteus's trying to grab the wedding ring, which had required the intervention of David and the Dean before he realised that the attempt was pointless. After that he had been curiously quiet; David thought he even looked relieved.

The Master looked deflated, too, all the pomposity leached out of him, as if the speed of events and the appalling truth were far too much for him to cope with.

All David wanted now was an explanation, but they were waiting for the police. Gawaine had asked for Father Gerard, too, and the Dean had phoned, before finding a seat near the French windows and muttering over his pipe.

Gawaine, sunk deep in one of the over-stuffed armchairs, was motionless except for the fingers of one hand beating a nervous rhythm on the arm. In a few moments all the remaining suspects would be assembled – with one exception.

"Don't you want Heatherington?" David asked.

Gawaine gave him an unexpectedly cold look. "I fail

to see, my dear David, that any useful purpose could be served by his presence at this point."

Before David could reply, a knock at the door announced the arrival of Father Gerard. Inspector Carter was hard on his heels, with the woman sergeant who had come with him to college to take fingerprints. Verner brought them up to date in a few brief sentences.

The Chaplain fixed Gawaine with a look, exclaimed mildly, "My dear fellow!" and went to sit near Porteus.

Inspector Carter gave Gawaine a long stare. "You know this is highly irregular," he said. "We're strongly discouraged from doing this sort of thing in the police… but we're going to do it anyway."

He found an upright chair placed back against the wall, neatly hitched up the knees of his trousers, and sat. His sergeant stationed herself by the door. She started to slide out a small notebook, only to put it away again at a gesture from the Inspector.

"Fire away," Carter said.

Gawaine took a deep breath. This was the moment he hated, David knew, but once launched, he would go on until everything was made clear. Physically frail, apparently ineffectual, he was still in control.

Everyone's attention was fixed on him; it occurred to David that Colonel Morrison might have appreciated hearing the truth about the murder he had so nearly been arrested for, but it was obviously impossible to wait until he could be dragged back from his family idyll in North Oxford.

"The confusing factor," Gawaine began, "is that there were not one, but two sequences of crime going on in College, connected, of course, but with separate motivation, and, it goes without saying, separate perpetrators. Once I realised that, the various anomalies over alibis and fingerprints disappear."

That might have been evident to him, but it was not evident to David, nor, he could guess, to any of the other listeners.

"I shall begin," Gawaine continued, "with what I suppose would be considered the lesser of the two crimes, although personally…however." He paused briefly, resisting the temptation to be side-tracked. "The first thought that gave me any sort of insight into what had happened was when I tried to imagine what Sue would have done when she arrived in college."

Porteus looked startled, and the Dean rumbled, "Sue?"

David intervened with a swift explanation. "The dead girl."

Gawaine glanced at him in acknowledgement. "She had never been to the college before," he went on. "That was self-evident, as otherwise someone might have had an idea of who she was, and might well have remembered when the bones came to light. She didn't know her way around, but she had come to visit the father of her unborn child, and as far as she was concerned, there was no reason for making a secret of it."

He raised a hand as the Dean seemed about to interrupt. "If that point bothers you, Dr Verner, I'll come back to it shortly. Under those circumstances, what would she do? She needs information, she needs to know where she can find the man she's come to see, and so – she goes to the porter's lodge."

He paused. There was an almost audible clicking as scholarly brains examined the implications of that.

"Heatherington," David murmured.

Gawaine favoured him with an edgy smile. "Precisely, my dear David. Heatherington. There is, of course, no proof that he happened to be on duty in the lodge on the day that Sue arrived, but I think we can infer it. What do we know of Heatherington?"

"Pain in the neck," muttered the Dean.

"We need to define him more exactly. Nosy, prone to gossip, and with a news-gathering service second to none. Now, if on that day another porter had been in the lodge when a young woman, obviously pregnant, came to inquire for Dr So-and-so – " David noticed he was still refusing to use a name – "would not the other porter take this juicy titbit to Heatherington, and it would subsequently be all round College. Which it was not."

"But if Heatherington – " David began, before he realised it might be better not to interrupt.

"As always, my dear David, you precede me. If Heatherington himself had been on duty, he also would have spread the gossip all round College – unless he already had a very good reason for keeping quiet." He stopped and took a breath. "Have you any reason to suspect, gentlemen, that Heatherington steams open the College mail?"

That question did not cause the shock that David might have expected.

"Shouldn't be at all surprised," the Dean replied, still struggling to get his pipe to light. "Wondered once or twice, in fact. No proof, or I'd have had him out."

The Master opened his mouth as if to voice an expostulation, then obviously thought better of it, and closed it again.

Gawaine nodded thoughtfully, as David recalled seeing Heatherington in the lodge, with the kettle whistling cosily away in the background. Had they almost caught him at it?

"Now if, in steaming open the mail," Gawaine resumed, "purely to satisfy his own curiosity, he should come across a piece of information that the letter's recipient really would not want known – might he not yield to the temptation to blackmail?"

"I sincerely hope – " Father Gerard began, to be cut off by Verner. "Damn' right he would."

"A college servant?" the Master protested. "Unthinkable!"

"Better start thinking it, Master," the Dean growled, triumphantly puffing at last. "Because if I'm any judge, we'll be looking for a new Head Porter."

Father Gerard made a helpless gesture, but he let the Dean's judgement stand. Porteus, staring broodingly at nothing, passed no judgement at all. David realised that none of this was any surprise to him.

Gawaine resettled himself in the armchair, glanced at David, and then began to speak again. David thought that he was growing tired, though the consciously didactic manner hid it effectively.

"At this point, gentlemen, I must tell you about a piece of evidence that came into my possession and subsequently was handed on to the police, though its true implications I only realised yesterday."

He went on to speak about Sue's letter, explaining about Marcia Scott's visit, though he said little about the contents of the letter in detail.

"The only relevant fingerprints on the letter," he concluded, "were Heatherington's and Templeman's own, which led us for a long time into believing that Heatherington must have been the father of the baby. Since he had, quite fortuitously, an alibi for the murder of Templeman, that assumption brought us up against a quite insurmountable brick wall. However, if we accept the idea of Heatherington as blackmailer, the fingerprint situation becomes quite clear. At the time he handled it, its real recipient had never seen it. Perhaps Heatherington sent on the rest of the letter, perhaps he kept it as evidence, but in some way, accidentally, that last page became separated, and was found by Templeman."

Gawaine turned to Father Gerard. "He came to you, did he not, and spoke of 'something discreditable going on in College', of which he had no definite proof?"

Father Gerard nodded. He had taken off his glasses and was polishing away vigorously, as if he had actually forgotten what he was doing.

"I thought at the time it was a poor way of describing murder," Gawaine went on. "In fact, what he was referring to was the blackmail, and possibly, in addition, the reason for which the blackmail took place."

Father Gerard let out a deep sigh. "Then I blame myself," he said. "I discouraged him from speaking about it, without proof. If I had…" He fell silent.

"Look here," the Dean began, preventing Gawaine from saying anything in reply, "this is all very well, St

Clair, I appreciate your reasoning, but that's all it is so far, reasoning. It could have happened that way, but you've given us no proof, no more than poor Templeman. What about a bit of hard evidence?"

"Yes," the Master agreed. "So far, this is all unsubstantiated – "

"All right," Gawaine murmured, cutting him off. "I was coming to that. When I read that scrap of Sue's letter, the first thing that struck me was how happy she sounded. She was looking forward to having her baby, and she was convinced that the man she was writing to would be looking forward to it just as much as she was. It took me a while to realise it, but it seems to me that there's only one set of circumstances that would explain that. I suspect it's true even today, and it was certainly true thirty years ago. And I did find hard evidence of that just now, when I searched Dr Porteus's rooms." He took out the wedding ring, which he had slipped into a pocket. "She would only have that kind of confidence if she was already his wife."

Chapter Twenty-Five

'...a distracted Conscience here, is a shadow or introduction unto Hell hereafter.'

Religio Medici

David thought that Gawaine possibly had too rosy a view of the married state, even thirty years ago, but he said nothing. His assumption had led him to the right conclusion, after all.

Gawaine leaned forward. "Dr Porteus," he said softly, "was I right about Heatherington?"

After a long moment, Porteus nodded. "I seem to have under-estimated your acumen, St Clair," he said with a thin smile.

Gawaine let out a breath and lay back. "Will you tell us?" he asked. His voice was quiet; if he had ever thought of Porteus as his enemy – which David doubted – he was showing no sign of triumph now.

And after another long moment, Dr Porteus began.

"Sue and I were students together, in Manchester. We married early. I started work on my doctorate, and she did a teaching certificate and then got a job. And towards the end of three years I was writing up my thesis and looking for a university post. And then there was the baby."

Somehow he sounded entirely unlike Porteus as

David had come to know him. He was speaking quietly, simply, and as if it was a relief to get it off his chest. More people than Gawaine, David thought, might live behind a façade.

"We hadn't planned for a baby so soon," Porteus went on, "and that made it more important that I should get a good job. And I admit I was ambitious. I wanted this – an academic life." His lips twisted bitterly. "There weren't many possibilities. I saw the Griffin Fellowship advertised, and I knew – I knew that I had the ability to get it, but there was that damnable clause – the Fellow had to be unmarried. At first I hadn't thought it out, but I sent in an application anyway. I told myself that they might waive the rule for the right candidate, but I think right from the beginning I was deceiving myself, because I didn't mention Sue on my *curriculum vitae*. And I said nothing about it to Sue."

He hesitated, but no-one said anything to fill the silence. They were all too intent on what he had to say.

"By the time I was interviewed," he continued, "I'd been turned down for one or two other jobs, and I was getting worried. It looked as if I had a choice, between the Griffin Fellowship and leaving academic life altogether."

He drew a hand through his hair, and the ruffled appearance it left behind somehow brought the young, ambitious student vividly into the room.

"They offered it to me, and I accepted. Back then, no one did background checks on the internet, so I thought I had a good chance of getting away with it. I'd still said nothing to Sue. I knew she wouldn't have had anything to do with it. She was honest. She would rather have seen me washing dishes for a living than taking that Fellowship under false pretences."

"But for God's sake!" the Dean burst out. "How could you hope to keep it a secret from your wife for three years?"

Porteus shrugged. "I wasn't thinking that far ahead. It looked as if I could begin well enough. We were buying a house in Manchester, and the thought of a move – buying and selling, and packing up everything – would have been too much for Sue, in the final stages of pregnancy, and then with a small baby. We talked it over, and I managed to convince her to stay in Manchester, while I would live in college and come home whenever I could manage the time. I thought that would give me at least a year before she raised the question of moving again, and – well, I didn't think too much about what I would do then. Perhaps tell her the truth. I thought if I had a year's work behind me, she might agree to accept the situation. All that really mattered to me was to get my foot on the first rung of the ladder."

"Appalling!" the Master exclaimed, but no one paid any attention.

Porteus stopped speaking, and stared in front of him as if he was looking back over thirty years.

"So you took up the Fellowship..." Gawaine prompted softly.

"Yes. And for a few weeks all went well. But Sue wrote to me, naturally, and she knew no reason for hiding our relationship in her letters to me. And, as you said, Heatherington steams open the mail. I hadn't been in College very long before he paid me a visit – very apologetic, very ingratiating, but really, he did feel it was his duty to tell the

College authorities what was going on." There was a flash of the old, arrogant Porteus. "I paid him. What else could I do but pay him? And he kept quiet. And then the thing I'd never expected happened – Sue decided to visit me.

"She turned up outside my rooms, escorted by Templeman. He gave me a very odd look, but he didn't say anything, not in front of Sue. She told me she wanted to give me a surprise. All I could think of was how many people had seen her, and did they know who she was. Apparently she'd inquired for me at the lodge, but then she'd got lost, and asked Templeman for directions, and he showed her the way. She couldn't understand what was the matter with me. I couldn't see any way out of it. I told her the truth, that I'd been given the Fellowship on the assumption that I was unmarried.

"Sue was furious. I'd known she would be. She told me what I was doing was dishonest, and I should admit it and resign. I wish to God I had! But I refused, I asked her how she thought I was going to support her and the baby, because no other university would ever give me a job once they knew what I'd done. All I wanted was for her to go, so that no-one else would see her, and I could think of what I was going to tell Templeman. And she walked out. She said I could come home once I'd resigned the Fellowship, but otherwise she didn't want to see me again. I argued – I didn't want her to go like that – I knew she couldn't look after the baby properly on her own. But she walked out.

"I swear I never touched her. She rushed out of my rooms, tripped, and fell down the stairs. When I got to her she was dead. I didn't kill her. I loved her. I would never have hurt her."

"But you buried her out there!" the Dean said.

"Yes. I was kneeling beside her at the bottom of the stairs. Part of me couldn't believe she was dead. But part of me was thinking that if I could get rid of her body, I could still keep the job. I couldn't report her death as an accident, because the first thing I would have to say about her would be that she was my wife. At least, if I could keep her death quiet, I was finally entitled to the Fellowship, because I wasn't a married man any longer."

"Dear Heaven!" Verner breathed out.

"I don't know what I would have done, because just at that moment Heatherington came along. It was he who had spoken to Sue in the lodge. He had just come off duty, and although he didn't say so, he had come round for a snoop. He found me with her body. I don't think for one minute he believed me when I told him that I hadn't killed her. But he offered to help me… dispose of her. Of course, my contributions would have to increase…

"I couldn't see what else to do. If I confessed, I could see that I stood a good chance of being tried for her murder. So we hid her body in my rooms until that night, and then we buried her in the gardens."

"Where she stayed until they broke ground for the library extension," Verner remarked. "Good God! I've just remembered – you opposed building that extension. You said it wasn't necessary."

"Indeed," Gawaine commented, very quiet and expressionless. "An oversight on my part. I should have asked if anyone had seemed unwilling for the garden to be disturbed."

More practically, David interposed, "Did nobody ask about her? What about her family?"

Sunk in reflection, Porteus seemed not to have heard the question. Then suddenly he jerked, and replied, "Sue's parents were dead, and there was no other close family. And her home was in the north, a long way from here. A few friends wrote to her for a while, and I sent cards at Christmas for a year or two… I sold up our house in Manchester. I told my own family Sue had left me, and they accepted that."

Gawaine shivered, and even David felt a touch of chill at the thought of Sue's life, so easily blotted out.

It was the Dean who asked, "What about Templeman?"

Porteus looked at him without seeing him. "I spoke to Templeman the next day. I told him that the woman – Sue – had been annoying me, pretending that she was married to me to stir up trouble, when I wasn't even sure that I was the baby's father. I said I'd given her some money and she'd gone. He believed me, though he didn't look happy about it, and he never mentioned her again, until her body was found.

"I lied when I said I hadn't seen Templeman that morning. He came to see me – he said he wanted to give me a reprint of his latest paper, but that wasn't all he had on his mind."

David flashed a look at Gawaine, but Gawaine, brooding, was unaware of it.

"He also told me about the bones in the garden," Porteus went on, "and he accused me outright of knowing something about them. I denied it, but he wanted me to go to you, Dean, and confess. 'Make a clean breast of it,' he said." A sneering look crossed Porteus's face. "A clean breast, after thirty years! Then he said he would go to the Dean himself. I panicked. I could see it all coming out. As he left my rooms I followed him, and pushed him. He fell down the stairs, just as Sue did."

"And you put him in the trunk room," Verner said.

"Not right away. I hadn't a key. I dragged him back into my rooms. Then I tried to get hold of Heatherington, but he wasn't in college."

"And now we know why he left," Gawaine murmured. "He would realise everything was going to come out. No wonder he went home where he could think it out quietly."

Porteus went on as if he had not spoken. "I saw him later, and I made it quite clear to him that he had to help me again. If what I'd done came out, I wouldn't keep quiet about the blackmail. He had to agree, but it was difficult to know what to do. We couldn't start digging in the garden again. In the end we put him in the trunk room – Heatherington has keys, of course – hoping to do something more permanent when things had quietened down. Most of the dons who were leaving for the vacation had already left, so there wasn't much reason for anyone to go down there."

He sighed deeply, and dropped his head into his hands. He went on speaking, but more indistinctly now. "I'm glad it's over. I keep thinking back, to that first decision I made, to accept the Fellowship. It all came from that. I've got what I wanted, the academic career, the success, the respect. But if I'd chosen differently, I'd have had Sue, and our children."

In the silence that followed, David heard Father

Gerard murmur softly, "What shall it profit a man, if he gain the whole world, and lose his own soul?"

Gawaine broke the next silence that fell, turning to Inspector Carter, who had sat silently listening throughout the long explanation, only following each point with that patient, all-seeing gaze. "Inspector, yesterday I suggested that you look into Heatherington's bank account," he said. "There should be evidence of blackmail payments, and corresponding withdrawals from Dr Porteus's account. And I imagine you'll be able to inquire among Manchester dentists for Susan Porteus's dental records. That will – " He broke off. "I'm sorry," he went on after a moment. "You know all this, of course."

Inspector Carter nodded. "Of course. And you and I will need to have a talk, but not just yet." He rose and went over to Porteus, who stood up to meet him.

Gawaine turned away sharply, as if he didn't want to see or hear what would happen next.

As David heard Inspector Carter begin to give Porteus the standard caution, he got up and stood over Gawaine's chair. Gawaine had completely lost the air of spurious authority with which he had explained his reasoning. He looked exhausted, and the blue eyes he raised to David were blank and terrified.

David bent over him. "Let's get out of here," he suggested.

Chapter Twenty-Six

'No man can justly censure or condemn another, because indeed no man truly knows another.'
Religio Medici

They ended up on the bench in the Delphinium Walk, where almost two weeks earlier they had sat to discuss possible suspects. David remembered that conversation vividly; Gawaine had been almost enjoying himself. He was not enjoying himself now. It had all become real since then.

David would have liked to remove himself and his friend from Oxford right away, but he knew they had one more conversation to go with the police before they would be allowed to leave. Meanwhile, he respected Gawaine's silence. He was leaning back with one hand covering his eyes, and he was shivering. David had seen this reaction before, wretchedly miserable once the tension had relaxed, and eventually he realised it was time to start pulling him out of it.

There was only one sure way of doing that.

"Look," he said. "There's a lot you haven't explained yet. Who stabbed you, for a start?"

He went through a nasty moment when he thought Gawaine was not going to answer. Then his friend turned to face him with a faint, apologetic smile. "Oh, that was Heatherington, of course," he replied, "though I doubt the police will ever bring it home to him. It couldn't have been Porteus, because as Seff found out, he has an alibi. Heatherington was in Chapel, and he saw me there. And he'd seen those notes of Seff's. Remember, he was a blackmailer, and an accessory to what as far as he was concerned were two murders. If Porteus was caught, then it was the end for Heatherington, too. As, of course, it will be."

There was an undeniable trace of satisfaction in Gawaine's voice. David could understand that, and share it.

"Thirty years," Gawaine went on dreamily. "Thirty years living in sight of the spot where you buried your wife. And being blackmailed on the strength of it. I hope he only gets a short sentence. He's served one already."

Momentarily, David was surprised he could be so charitable, especially if Porteus had been responsible for his own breakdown. Then, thinking it over, he was not surprised at all, but he could not risk asking, "Was he any good at his job?"

"Brilliant."

"He didn't do you much good, did he?"

Gawaine's brows arched in the familiar expression of well-bred astonishment. David, conscious of having ventured too far, waited for the inevitable, if aristocratic, put-down.

Instead, after a brief pause, Gawaine relaxed. "That's all nonsense. Porteus drove his students, but if you were worth anything, you could take it. He drove himself."

"And now we know why."

"Yes. He sold his soul for his job. He had to make a success of it."

His tragic look was gathering again, and David hastily added, "But it sounds as if Templeman did it better."

Gawaine nodded slowly. "That's very perceptive. Templeman and the Dean, at that time, were…very good. That's the main reason I felt I had to do this."

"But you haven't told me – " David was determined to battle his way out of these deep waters – "why you knew it was Porteus in the first place. You knew you were going to find that wedding ring."

Gawaine nodded again, but this time more briskly; as David had hoped, the intellectual effort was bringing him back to normal.

"If she was married, as I assumed, there had to be a ring. It wasn't with her. I assumed further that if her husband had loved her, he would have kept it." For a few seconds his gaze unfocused, and he repeated in a whisper, "He would have kept it…"

"But why Porteus?" David demanded.

"He had the most to lose if he were found to be married. I couldn't accept Heatherington as a bigamist – to run two establishments you have to be able to move around, and he was tied to College. I also couldn't accept Father Gerard as being secretly married. It is, I suppose, just conceivable that he might have got a girl pregnant, but marrying her without coming out into the open implies a whole new order of hypocrisy. Also there was no reason for him not to own her. He could even have continued as Chaplain. The Dean, I admit, was approaching marriage with the bishop's daughter – but I couldn't accept that he was contemplating bigamy either. He would have known that it couldn't last, and again, he wasn't sufficiently mobile. And Morrison was still an undergraduate, several years away from marriage with the present Mrs Morrison. He could have owned Sue as his wife, and they would probably have found their families and the College quite helpful over the imminent baby.

"But Porteus – first of all, he'd come from outside Oxford, and no-one at that time knew much about him. And as I said, he had too much to lose. The Griffin Fellowship, the prospect of an academic job anywhere else – and probably legal proceedings to face if they found out that he'd accepted the Fellowship under false pretences. His whole career would have been wrecked. And then there was the question of his name."

David thought back. "Oh, yes…what was it? Miles John. And the baby was going to be John."

Gawaine gave him an innocent look that suggested he was about to drop a neat bombshell. "Not only that, my dear David. Remember Sue's letter – 'a soldier like his Dad'? Unfortunately we had a soldier on our list of suspects, which wasted a lot of time and effort. But it wasn't the baby's profession Sue was talking about, it was his name. And Porteus's name is Miles, or in Latin, *miles*, a soldier. The word, of course, from which we derive 'military'. I was very close, though I didn't know it, when I was quoting Ovid. It was no surprise at all when Porteus told us Sue was a classicist too."

He looked positively smug. David, brain whirling, was quite prepared to look like an idiot if it meant that

Gawaine cheered up. Besides, he comforted himself, no one but a student of Latin could have been expected to pick that one up.

Half a minute later, Gawaine's smug expression vanished. He was looking at something over David's shoulder, and David turned to see the Dean approaching.

"Inspector Carter would like a word," Verner announced as soon as he was in earshot. "Will you come and talk to him?"

"Yes, of course, Dean," Gawaine replied, colourlessly correct.

"Porteus will co-operate with the police," Verner went on. "He'd damn' well better. College will do its best for him, of course. As for Heatherington…" He shrugged. "My room in ten minutes."

He was about to go, and then swung round again. "Come back. You've got the scholar's mind, St Clair. Come back."

Gawaine looked up at him, and David could have sworn he considered the possibility for about five seconds. Then, mutely, he shook his head. The Dean breathed heavily, glared at David, and finally gave up and stumped off.

Epilogue

Value the Judicious, and let not mere acquests in minor parts of Learning gain thy pre-existimation.

Christian Morals, II.iv

David pushed open the door of the wine bar and looked around. The working day was ending, and the place already beginning to fill up, though it took David only a moment to spot Seff Brown, waving at him from a booth at the back. He wove his way through the chattering crowd and slid into the seat opposite her.

"Hi," he said.

"Hi yourself," Seff responded, pushing a glass of red wine toward him with a bowl of nibbles.

David eyed the offerings warily. "To what do I owe this honour?"

"It's a glass of wine, David, not the Crown Jewels!" Seff said, raising her eyes exasperatedly. "And in case you were worried, my name isn't Borgia. I want some information, that's all."

"Information?" David picked up the glass of wine and took a sip. "What about?"

"Honestly…you know perfectly well what about."

David did. He had known ever since Seff's phone call earlier that afternoon. *There's only one reason she would ever ask me out for a drink.* He still wasn't sure what had possessed him to agree to meet her.

"Oxford," Seff continued when David made no response. "The police have made an arrest, and my paper was the only one without the story, because I was pulled off it. But no one knows the *inside* story – they probably don't realise there is one."

"And is there?" David asked, unable to resist baiting her.

"I'm not stupid!" Seff snapped. "Everyone else seems to assume that Gawaine dropped out of the investigation after he was attacked. But don't tell me that he wasn't involved in the arrest, and don't tell me that you weren't with him."

"Okay, I won't." By now Seff was looking dangerous; realising that he might be about to receive a glass of Merlot down his shirt front, David went on rapidly, "Calm down…I'll tell you what there is to tell."

He launched into the story of that last day in Oxford, how Gawaine had found the wedding ring that proved Porteus had taken the Fellowship under false pretences; how Sue had died accidentally, and Templeman when he confronted Porteus with his suspicions; how Heatherington had blackmailed Porteus for the last thirty years.

Completely focused, Seff took notes as he spoke. "It doesn't bear thinking about," she murmured as David finished. "Thirty years… I suppose it was Heatherington who stabbed Gawaine?"

David nodded. "Gawaine thinks so. And if the police can't get him for that, he'll do a good long stretch for the blackmail."

"Excellent. Nasty little toad." Seff snapped her notebook shut. "How is Gawaine?" she added. "Is he staying with you?"

"No, I took him home with me on the Saturday, after the police had finished with him, and he stayed over yesterday, but this morning he got the train home. I wish he hadn't, but I couldn't talk him out of it."

"I know..." Seff actually looked sympathetic, though David guessed her sympathy was for Gawaine rather than for him. "Somehow I get the impression that this time was more upsetting for him than usual."

There was a question in her voice, though she hadn't asked anything. David's first instinct was to say nothing. This was Gawaine's private business, an area where anyone who knew him should tread very carefully, if at all.

Then on deeper reflection he realised that if he said nothing, Seff might well put her foot in it, either in print or when she next met Gawaine.

"This has to be off the record," he said.

Seff picked up her notebook and stowed it away in the messenger bag on the seat beside her. "Entirely off the record," she agreed, topping up their wine glasses.

"When Gawaine was a student at St Clement's," David told her, "he had a breakdown. I don't know what brought it on, but I do know that Porteus was his tutor."

Seff took a sip of wine. "Oh, yes, I can imagine tutorials with Porteus must have been a whole bunch of fun. So Gawaine never finished his degree?" she added. "I didn't know that."

"Verner thinks he should go back."

"And he won't?"

David shook his head. "Not a chance. Well, he doesn't need the degree, does he? He's perfectly okay down in Surrey with his books and his cats."

"I wonder…" Seff looked thoughtful. "How does he finance that, by the way? Does he have a secret life as a bank robber?"

David narrowly avoided snorting wine all over the table. "Family money, I suppose," he replied. "I haven't asked. It's none of my business." With a spurt of amused affection, he added, "It's just as well, though. I mean… would you employ him?"

"I don't know," Seff responded. "He might be very happy tucked away somewhere in a museum or a library. Happier than he is catching murderers."

"That's for sure," David said.

"Well…" Seff drained her wine glass and pushed the remains of the bottle over to David. "Finish that, if you like. I've got to get my story in. That'll teach Edwin Galbraith to try gagging me."

A warm feeling of satisfaction spread over David as he thought of how annoyed the Master would be when he read Seff's paper.

"Give my best to Gawaine," Seff said as she rose to her feet. "I'll see you both next time."

"Next time?" David frowned. "There's going to be a next time?"

"Oh, I think so, don't you? For Gawaine, there's always a next time. See you."

David turned and watched her out of the door, convinced in spite of his misgivings that she was right.